CW00404092

BECOMING HIS MATE: DOUGLAS MOUNTAIN SHIFTERS
FOUNTAIN OF LOVE

LILLIAN DANTÉ

ISBN-13: 978-1499138900
ISBN-10: 1499138903

TABLE OF CONTENTS

From the Author:

This story is a lot of things. It's my homage to stories about strong warriors confronting their destiny, star-crossed lovers, and fated mates. It's a love song. It's an adventure.

It's also my tribute to the Pacific Northwest.

While Alki Valley, Foxwoods, and the whole Douglas Mountain region as described in the story are fictional, they're based on the area where I grew up. As far as I know, there weren't any shifters living there - but I've been wrong before.

Most of all, though, it's something I hope will put a smile on your face.

Without you, the readers, nothing I do would be possible. So every book I write is sort of a love letter to the audience. If you can escape into this world for just a little while, just long enough to forget about the things you want to forget, and remember the things you want to remember - then I've done my job.

xoxo,
Lillian

P.S. If you can't get enough stories about magical and

mysterious fountains, please check out the rest of the books in the Fountain of Love series. *The Fountain of Love is Timeless. The Fountain of Love is Wonderful. The Fountain of Love is Magic. Join 15 authors as they spin the tale of the Fountain. The settings and characters may change, but the fountain will remain.* Like us on Facebook at **facebook.com/fountainromance**, and the visit the Fountain website at **fountainromance.com**. Every book in the Fountain series is available for free, exclusively on Amazon Kindle, for the first five days after release.

Chapter One

His fingers trailed down the side of my neck, leaving a tingling pathway on my skin. The ghost of a sensation I'd felt just moments ago. He had that effect on me. Always had. Probably always would. My body refused to forget his touch, refused to let go, no matter how hard I tried.

Not that I was trying particularly hard. Not right now. And I hated myself for that, but then his fingers dipped down, between my breasts, down my stomach, sliding under the waistband of my panties.

I forgot to hate myself. I forgot why I'd ever tried to resist him.

My nipples stiffened as I bit my lower lip, arching into his touch until I felt a twinge of protest in the muscles of my hips and ass.

Cole chuckled in my ear. I shivered at the sensation of his hot breath against the sensitive skin. "It always drives me crazy when you do that," he murmured. "Biting your lip, trying not to smile." He blew out a tiny puff of air, making me shiver and moan softly. "Failing."

Drives, he said. Present tense, like this was a thing we were still doing, had been doing all along - like we hadn't spent nine and half years as strangers trying to forget each other's existence. Like he hadn't run away right after high school graduation...

"Heather," Cole whispered. "Heather. Where are you?"

I bit my lip harder. "Right here," I insisted, and a moment later the dip of his fingers made it true. Memories scattered in my mind like so many dandelion seeds in the wind. His teeth scraped against my earlobe, gently, and my whole body shuddered in response.

"I don't believe you," he whispered, his fingers curling deeper. "Well. Maybe now I do." His lips were curved up in a smile, all wickedness and sin.

I sighed, feeling myself melt and surrender to him completely. My inner muscles clenched around his fingers as he stroked against that particular spot deep inside.

"You haven't changed a bit," I murmured, absently.

He grinned. His teeth glinted in the moonlight shining through the window, and I felt an inexplicable shiver of fear in the pit of my stomach.

"I think I have," he said. "Never found *this* before, did I?"

He punctuated with another stroke, and I shuddered.

"No," I moaned, my head arching back into my pillow. "But I don't remember complaining."

A moment later his thumb joined in, rubbing little circles on the stiff nub at the top of my sex. Shuddering, I gave in.

This wasn't part of the plan. When I let him spend the night in my house, this wasn't supposed to happen. I was going to be strong.

But I never felt stronger than when I was in his arms. I might be weak now, as my climax overtook me - but in a little while, I'd have him reduced to a similar state, shuddering and needy inside of me. It was all part of the give and take. It was beautiful. It was fucking terrifying.

Moaning and convulsing under his fingers, every part of my body tingling with pleasure, I forgot everything. The only thing that mattered was us. This moment. Pure bliss.

When I opened my eyes, he was still smiling.

"You're gonna be the death of me," I whispered.

As it turned out, I was almost right.

On the day Cole came back, everything seemed ordinary at first. But isn't that always the way? Wake up, gulp down some coffee, take your meds, shuffle through your morning routine. Nothing's memorable - until suddenly, something is.

It was like that.

I got to work early, like always, and spent a while sitting behind the counter and yawning before I sorted through the keys in the overnight drop-off box.

"Hey, Heather - what's the blue Cobalt? Oil change or something?" My boss, Joe, was popping his head out through the connecting door into the garage.

"Wheel bearing," I said, handing him the key fob. "Sounds like it, anyway."

He nodded, disappearing. I'd been working the front desk at Joe's Automotive since high school, and I'd picked up just enough car know-how to avoid embarrassing myself. Some women might wrinkle their nose at the idea, but I don't mind being surrounded by the testosterone all day. These guys had known me since I was a kid, and I had a feeling most of them wouldn't hesitate to help me bury a body.

Not that I ever would. You know. It's a figure of speech.

We had the advantage of being very close to Foxwoods, the massive planned community with houses so far out of my price range, I felt myself get poorer just by *looking* at them. The residents would bring in their fancy sedans because it was the cheapest tow, but Joe's honesty, fairness and lightning-fast repairs kept them coming back.

We had plenty of customers from Alki Valley, too. They were my favorites. Well, maybe it's more accurate to say that the

Foxwoods people were my *least* favorite, and everything else shone by comparison. But even on the worst days, it was never too bad. Joe and the others would always have my back when an irate customer got out of hand. That was more than I could say for most retail jobs.

While I sat there, sorting through some parts orders from the day before, a subtle scent made my nose twitch. On a conscious level I couldn't have identified it, but the flood of feelings and memories filled in the blanks for me.

Cole.

I looked up, my heart pounding like a snare drum. It was totally irrational; no one could get in or out of this tiny room without my knowing about it. He wasn't here. The smell was a phantom. Like everything else involving Cole, it was just a flight of fancy. Nothing real.

All the same, I couldn't focus on the my work again until I'd poked my head through the connecting door to make sure he hadn't suddenly materialized in the garage. The instinct was too strong to ignore. Every part of my body, from my racing pulse to the goosebumps on my skin to the hairs on the back of my neck, standing stiff, was convinced of one thing.

He was nearby.

I shook my head at my own stupidity and sat back down, trying hard to squash the memories.

I hadn't seen Cole Jackman in almost ten years. He left Alki Valley in his rear-view right after high school graduation, and by then, I'd lost my right to cry for him. His girlfriend Dani cried instead, but instead of vicious triumph, I felt a stab of jealousy.

Which was, in fact, balls-out *crazy*. But I never claimed I was sane.

Not when it came to Cole, anyway.

And this was just more proof of that. My eyes kept scanning over the same line of numbers over and over again, but I couldn't understand them. The roots of my hair still tingled.

"Heather?" It was a voice from behind my shoulder. I almost jumped out of my skin.

"Sorry." Steve was chuckling as he walked in, wiping his hands. "Didn't mean to startle you."

"I wasn't," I lied, briskly rubbing my upper arms to calm the goosebumps. "Just got absorbed in, uh…" I glanced down at my desk. "…this stuff."

"Sure." Steve was smiling, but he looked a little concerned. He wasn't going to push it, though. That was one of the many things I liked about him. That, and the fact that he and his wife put me up in their furnished basement apartment for about half of what they could've charged, on the open rental market.

"Did you see the paper today?" he asked, patting where it sat on the desk.

"Not yet." I hadn't even glanced at it. I usually didn't, unless someone tipped me off to a particularly juicy story. The local news was seldom interesting, and often irritating.

"They're talking about developing the woods," he said, tapping on a particular headline. "Selling off the land to the highest bidder."

I sighed. "They talk about that every year. And every year, nothing changes."

"No, not like this," Steve insisted. "The new commissioner is giving statements about it. Look."

Frowning, my strange interlude with the phantom smell all but forgotten, I picked up the paper and began to read.

Anyone who's hiked the five-mile trail that connects the Foxwoods housing development to Alki Valley will tell you how beautiful it is. The old-growth pines and mossy boulders give a home to countless species of wildlife, while the old fountain marks a perfect halfway point to enjoy a picnic lunch on your way through. For decades, the land that it bisects has been state property. But with the recent departure of County Commissioner Lane Watkins, new questions have been raised about the land's future.

While it costs the state little to maintain the trails, relying mostly on volunteer labor, the sale of the land could bring in a significant amount of revenue.

"It's certainly nothing to sneeze at," new Commissioner Wanda Pollitt says. "We're very mindful of the importance of maintaining our area's natural beauty, and it's not a decision we'd make lightly. But the fact is, the land is highly desirable, and the demands on our state budget increase every year. Everyone wants the best of all worlds: well-maintained trails and parks, perfect schools, smooth roads - but realistically, something has to give. If the residents of the area can learn to live without the trail, the benefits could be wide-reaching."

During his tenure, former Commissioner Watkins was determined to keep the land preserved in its natural state. At the time of this article, he could not be reached for comment.

The article continued on the next page, but I only scanned the words, looking for another mention of the fountain. There was none.

"I know what you're about to ask," said Steve. "And no, there's no guarantee the fountain wouldn't be part of the sale. God knows what would happen to it."

"That's insane." My stomach clenched with anger. "How can they even talk about this?"

Steve let out a bitter laugh. "I'll do you one better. Guess who's backing the plan to sell?"

My jaw dropped. "No," I said. "You've got to be kidding me."

He shook his head. "Afraid not. The Foxwoods community board just made their statement. They're all in favor."

"This is insane." I rubbed my temples, staring down at the paper without really seeing it. "I really think I'm losing my mind. Or maybe this whole county is."

"Could be," Steve grunted, flopping down in one of the chairs we kept for customers. "But there's no way Alki Valley will let this happen."

"There's no way they'll be able to stop it," I countered. "Nobody loves the fountain as much as politicians love money."

"Ain't that the sad truth." Steve grinned ruefully, sticking his legs out in front of him. "Still. I think Alki might surprise you."

I wanted to believe him, but I wasn't sure I could. The rivalry between Foxwoods and Alki Valley was bitter and long-standing, but Alki lacked the organization and resources to fight the sale of the land.

Officially, both places weren't part of any town or city. They existed in a no-man's land of unincorporated county property, which meant they were subject to the leadership of politicians who rarely, if ever, set foot in our neck of the woods. We had no local representation in the government. I'd grown up listening to the murmurs of discontent, but until now, I'd never found a reason to get angry about it.

The bell on the door jingled, and both Steve and I looked up.

"Do you have time for an oil change?" asked a melodious voice that I immediately recognized. I smiled, looking up.

"Adanna, how are you?"

She slipped into the room, swaying up to my desk with her usual dancer's posture. "Very well, thank you. I haven't had a chance to call for an appointment - I'm so sorry."

"No trouble at all, Ms. Ogbuagu." Steve stood up, brushing his hands on his pants. "Keys?"

Alki Valley didn't really have an official leadership structure, but when we were kids, Cole's father had acted as a sort of de-facto one-man community board. Everyone seemed comfortable going to him for advice, and he did a good job speaking for the rest of us whenever we needed a voice in county affairs. Shortly after graduation, he'd decided to retire to Florida with his wife.

Adanna moved to town right after that - a fortunate coincidence, as she turned out to be the perfect replacement. Stepping into his shoes effortlessly, she'd become one of the most beloved members of our community.

"I guess you must've seen the paper," I said, as I filled out her claim check.

Her expression clouded over. "I spent all morning on hold with the commissioner's office," she said. "Just to leave a message. This is the first I've heard of the whole thing. But see if you can guess who already knew about it - *and* gave the commissioner his blessing."

Shaking my head, I handed her an invoice. "I just heard - but to be fair, I probably could have guessed."

"Arthur's the next person on my 'to call' list," she said. "I'm almost going to enjoy it. Although I doubt I'll get anything productive out of him."

Arthur Craven was the community board leader of Foxwoods, self-appointed neighborhood watch captain, and regular contributor to the local paper's op-ed column. I couldn't be in his presence without developing a persistent eyelid twitch.

"I'm sorry," I said. "If it helps, just remind yourself about the time he called the cops to his house because there was a raccoon walking across his pool cover."

Adanna's laugh was musical and infectious, filling the small room.

"Oh, Heather. You always know what to say." She smiled, and as always, it had that certain Mona Lisa quality about it. "I'll see you in about an hour?"

"Sounds good."

Business picked up over the next few hours, and I didn't have much time to dwell on my strange morning. It wasn't until we closed up for the evening that I started to think about everything again. Cole. His scent. His face, the way I remembered it. The fountain.

"You want a ride home?" Steve asked me, like he did every night. I shook my head.

"No thanks," I said. "It's nice out."

"You sure? I hear there's a dangerous prowler around." He grinned. Even though crime in these parts was rarer than a bigfoot sighting, people still found a way to get whipped up into a frenzy about "suspicious" strangers. I felt bad for anyone who got lost and pulled into a driveway to check their GPS - most likely, they'd end up photographed and posted on the "NEIGHBORHOOD WATCH" board at the Foxwoods community clubhouse.

"I'll take my chances," I told him, smiling. "Thanks, though."

Tonight, more than ever, I wanted to walk. The remains of summer weather were still clinging stubbornly to the early autumn, and I wouldn't have many more opportunities to enjoy the trip home without getting rained on.

And tonight, more than ever, I wanted to see the fountain.

It wasn't directly on my way home, but I often stopped by anyway, taking a short detour into the woods. As a kid I'd come to make wishes, but nowadays I knew better. All the same, I liked it. Spending time by the fountain always seemed to quiet my mind.

When I was with Cole, I never brought him here. He never tried to bring me, either. We never discussed it, but I was grateful. Even when things were the most heated between us, and we hardly wanted to be apart, I still needed this place to be mine. I needed a place to go that had no traces of him.

Once he left me, I needed the fountain more than ever. Many nights of my senior year, its cool, clear water mingled with my tears. But when I left, my eyes were always dry.

Leaving through the back door in the garage, I made my way to the wooded path that would take me where I wanted to go.

The sun wasn't even setting yet, but the thick foliage made the way seem dusky-dark and full of secrets.

I closed my eyes, and took a deep breath.

Enjoy it while it lasts.

Visions of high-rise condos and shopping malls flashed before my eyes, but even those worries faded as I walked. Fallen pine needles crunched beneath my feet, releasing their pungent, Christmasy scent into the air.

There was a soft rustling noise from just off the path. I stopped and peered towards it, finally spotting an expanse of tawny fur that was well-hidden in the underbrush.

"Hi," I whispered, meeting the glint of his eyes with my own. "I don't want any trouble, buddy." He remained motionless as I stared at him. After a moment, I turned back to the path and continued on my way. I didn't hear any more noises, but all the same, I knew the cougar was following me. They always did. The first few times, when I was a kid, it scared me half to death. But soon enough, I realized they were just curious. Cougar sightings were common enough around here, but I sometimes wondered if they took a particular interest in me - or if I was just more observant than most people. I didn't know anyone else who claimed to be followed as often as I was.

Large predators, in particular, seemed to have an affinity for me. I didn't mind, so long as they had no intention of turning me into a meal. Whatever drew them to me in the first place, it didn't seem to be a sense that I was any kind of threat. Even when I'd walked right up to a bear cub when I was young, and didn't know any better, his mother just came and quietly nudged him back to the woods. I stood there, little eight-year-old me, frozen with fear, but the mother bear just snuffled curiously in my direction and let me be. I knew better than to tell my parents, if I ever wanted to be allowed to play in the woods again.

I could hear the fountain in the distance. I quickened my pace, but not too much. The last thing I needed was for the cougar to think I was trying to run away. I might have "a way with animals," but I wasn't going to push my luck.

He wouldn't follow me for much longer. Wild animals never lingered by the fountain for long. Nobody knew why, because it wasn't dangerous. At least, not in any way that we could understand.

The thing about the fountain is that it's hard to explain.

It's one of those things that you sort of have to accept from a young age, or it's always going to bother you. Like a lot of local legends and traditions, it doesn't make sense. It's unnerving to newcomers. I've tried to tell the story to other adults, the way it was told to me as a child, but it doesn't quite work.

When you first learn about the fountain, it helps if you still believe in magic. Even if it's just a little bit.

The thing about the fountain is, nobody knows how it got here.

Anyone who's not from Douglas Mountain would stop me right there. *How is that possible? It's not mentioned in any of the old records from the loggers and the early settlers? It can't even be all that old. I mean, look at it. Are you saying someone built that in secret? How? Where does the water come from?*

Once you've lived here for a while, you understand. We've studied the fountain as much as we can. There've been specialists from all over the country, but they've done everything they can do without damaging it. As far as we know, the water comes from a natural spring. The fountain's age is hard to determine. They can't get conclusive results from their testing, and after a while, we stopped letting them take samples. Even though the fountain never seems to show any wear and tear, we weren't taking any chances.

Of course, this was some time ago. Apparently, things had changed. Now there was actually discussion of selling this land -

for profit. Some of the old-timers, the people who'd lived here for generations, must be rolling over in their graves. But that was all they could do. Most of their children and their children's children had moved on, buying bigger houses in bigger developments, miles and miles away. They went and bought themselves waterfront property, somewhere like Bainbridge Island, and they never looked back.

More and more, there was no one left who really understood the fountain.

Not that we really *understood* it, in any traditional sense of the word. But even though I couldn't tell you where it came from, or how it was made, or how it worked - I understood the fountain.

I was reaching the clearing now. As clouds rushed past the waxing moon, it alternated between very light and very dark. But the fountain always shone, as if it were reflecting something. Even when there seemed to be no light anywhere.

When did it get dark? I haven't been walking that long.

I'd never been afraid before. Not in the presence of the fountain. But tonight, something felt strange. My hairs prickled on the back of my neck and my heart was starting to pound, harder and harder, and -

There it is again.

The smell.

Cole.

Hugging my arms tightly around my chest, I turned around so that the fountain was at my back. For some reason, I felt like nothing could approach me from that way. My eyes darted all over, hearing noises in the trees that I wasn't even certain were real. Pure panic rose in my throat.

"Hello, stranger."

I was wrong. Something *had* come from behind me, and it was now standing on the other side of the fountain.

And in the back of my mind, I was still trying hard to prove to myself that I didn't know exactly who it was. But this time, the smell was no ghost.

I turned around, slowly.

Cole Jackman. Still tall and lean, still with that stubble on his strong jaw, that short dark hair, those bright blue eyes. They always had a way of piercing right through me, and tonight was no different.

I should have relaxed, at least a little bit, but my body refused. My heart still hammered insanely fast as I stared at him. He was smiling - a little bit sheepishly. But not enough.

"What the *fuck*?" I snapped, glaring at him. "You should know better than to sneak up on a girl in the woods."

He raised both his hands, palms facing me. "I didn't mean to," he said. "I swear. Just got back in town, and I wanted to see the fountain."

"You don't give a shit about the fountain," I said, letting myself smile a little bit. It was hard not to, even while every fiber of my being screamed *RED ALERT*!

Was I always this jumpy? How could he still have such a profound effect on me?

"Course I do," he said, taking a cautious step towards me. "I'm from Douglas Mountain, after all."

Inch by inch, I forced my bunched-up shoulders to relax. "Sorry," I said. "I didn't mean…it's just been a weird night."

Cole shrugged. "You have every right to be mad," he said. "But I do care. I came back."

"Nine and a half years later," I pointed out. I took one long, deep breath, and made sure to exhale the whole thing. "What gives?"

And then, he broke out that crooked smile - the one that never failed to tear down all my defenses. I felt my body melt, my arms flopping down loosely by my sides, my jaw unclenching, my feet growing just a little more unsteady.

"Does a guy need a reason to come home for a visit?" he said - it was very clearly a *statement*, not a question, and he was using that voice again. The sweet-like-honey voice that nobody could resist. My skin tingled with far too many memories, ones I should have left behind long ago.

I swallowed hard. "After nine and a half years?" With an effort, I crossed my arms again. "Yeah. Maybe he does."

"Well, I'm sorry to disappoint you. But it's nothing juicy. Just wanted to come home." He took another step, and then a few more. "I gotta believe there's some tiny part of you that's happy to see me, Heather."

"Very tiny," I said, biting back a grin. "How'd you know it was me, from back there?"

Cole shrugged again. "Just did." He tapped the side of his index finger against his lips a few times, the way he did when he was trying to think of the right words. "That wasn't supposed to be an innuendo, by the way," he said.

"It never is, with you," I said, letting the grin come to life. "They just come naturally."

He grinned back. "So to speak."

This was dangerous territory. Nearly a decade, and a few minutes in Cole's presence was already sending me spiraling back to a person I never wanted to be again. I hadn't thought it was possible. The wanton, needy girl that had once cried over this man was gone. Gone. Dead and buried in the recesses of my mind. In places in my heart that he'd left paralyzed.

Except, not anymore. His presence was exactly the right brand of necromancy to bring that girl back to life, shouting and clawing and demanding satisfaction. *You buried me alive, you bitch. I'll never die. Not as long as Cole Jackman exists in this world, or any other.*

Ugh. What a melodramatic asshole I used to be.

A thunder clap interrupted the awkward silence. I jumped, feeling my hair stand on end again.

"That was close," Cole murmured, taking a step closer. "You should get indoors."

"Just me?" Lightning exploded in the sky, briefly illuminating the angles of his face.

He's just too god damn beautiful.

"I'll be fine," he said. "You better hurry."

"Where are you staying?" I demanded, planting my feet.

"Dunno," he mumbled. "It's not important. Seriously - you still live nearby here? You should go."

"Just a few shakes," I said. "Come on - don't be ridiculous. You can wait out the storm at my place."

He shifted from one foot to the other for a moment, until the next thunder clap rearranged both of our heartbeats.

"Okay," he said, finally. "If you're sure."

"Of course I'm sure," I said. "Now come on. Hurry."

Chapter Two

I would have done the same for anyone. Honest. Nobody deserved to be out in a dangerous storm, not even somebody who once broke my heart. My invitation had nothing to do with the way my body tingled just from being near him, in a way that had nothing to do with the very real electricity in the air.

I set off running, and he was hot on my heels, taking the little winding path that led straight to the back of Steve and Andrea's house. I had my own entrance, so I wouldn't have to answer any awkward questions about letting Cole spend the night. Not that they'd care. But I still didn't want to talk about it. I didn't even want to endure any knowing smiles.

It just wasn't like that anymore. I wouldn't let him past my defenses again. That was the kind of mistake you just don't make twice.

After the next crack, the rain broke through. We were both soaked instantly, and I suddenly felt the chill in the air that hadn't been evident before. The soft dirt turned to mud beneath our feet, and as I jumped to avoid a rock in the pathway, I felt myself start to slip.

Cole's hand closed around my arm before I could truly lose my footing, lifting me back up like I weighed nothing.

"You okay?" he asked.

I nodded, trying not to let his plastered-down hair remind me of the first time we showered together.

When we finally reached my door, we both huddled under the woefully inadequate awning while I fumbled with my keys. Getting inside was a relief, but it only served to highlight just how soaked we both were.

"Ugh," I said, wringing out my hair on the boot tray while Cole dripped onto the mat. "Just give me a second. I'll get you a towel."

"Take your time," he said. "Get yourself changed. I'll be okay." He glanced around, taking stock of the place. "So you're staying with Steve and Andrea, huh? They offered me this place back…before graduation." He'd almost said *before I left*. I could tell, but I didn't say anything - just nodded in acknowledgement.

Thankfully, there wasn't much to ruin down here. The tile floor didn't protest as I squelched across it, heading for the linen closet.

"Steve has some old clothes in the garage he was going to get rid of," I said, shuffling back over with the towel. "I'll just grab something for you. I'm sure he won't mind."

Particularly because I'm not going to tell him.

"Oh - thanks," Cole said, sounding surprised.

"What?" I laughed, rubbing my hair vigorously. "I'm a good hostess."

"You sure are," he said. "I didn't exactly expect a warm welcome when I came back."

This time, it was my turn to shrug. I went to the connecting door and ducked out into the garage, grabbing the first few things that I could find in the bags that were bound for Goodwill. There was the tiniest risk of running into one of my housemates, but thankfully they were both upstairs somewhere.

"Here you go." I shoved a bundle of clothes at Cole, then went to my own dresser to fetch something for myself. "I'll just be a second."

I took my time changing in the bathroom, finger-combing my damp hair and trying to imagine how Cole would see the woman in the mirror. All those times he'd called me beautiful, and I never quite believed him. Did he still think that? Did he ever? Or was he just a clever high school student trying to get laid, picking off the stragglers from the back of the herd?

That's unfair. Don't be so hard on him.

Was that present-day Heather talking, or high-school Heather? I couldn't tell anymore.

Oh, shit. I was in trouble.

The T.V. was on when I came back out, and I had to chuckle at Cole's frown as he flipped through the fuzzy channels.

"No cable?" he asked, rhetorically.

I shrugged. "What's the point? Everything's online now. Steve and Andrea invite me to their watching parties for everything that's good - plus they let me use their HBO Go password."

He made a disapproving noise, and kept on flipping. Thanks to the mountain, antenna and even satellite signals couldn't really reach us. Cable was the only option, and while I could have paid for an extra box on Steve and Andrea's account, I just never bothered with it. After all these years, I hadn't forgotten much about Cole - but I did admittedly forget about his T.V. addiction.

Watching him out of the corner of my eye, I had to smile. The worn-out, oversized Seahawks shirt and threadbare khakis weren't exactly his style, but he wore them surprisingly well. But of course, he wore everything well.

I shook my head, trying to focus on the headache-inducing static. Anything was better than letting my thoughts drift to Cole and his amazing body while he was sitting right here next to me.

Holy shit, he was sitting *right here next to me*.

I hadn't quite allowed myself to think about the full implications of this. The reality of him. Cole. He was back. He was *in my apartment*. My tiny, one-room apartment, where I'd touched myself countless times to memories of him.

My face flushed hot. I couldn't think about that now. Not now, when things were actually going okay between us, somehow, even though anger and lust were currently fighting it out inside my head, and I had no idea what *he* was thinking.

"So," he said, the rumble of his voice shaking me out of my thoughts. But not quite far enough. I swallowed hard, and looked at him, my pulse pounding.

"Yeah?" I said. "So, what?"

He half-smiled, and I melted a little more. "Tell me what I've missed. What's new in Alki Valley?"

For the first time since earlier in the day, I remembered the news story about the land sale. My forehead crinkled a little. "Nothing much," I said. "Except they're talking about selling that land between us and Foxwoods."

"No!" Cole's brown instantly furrowed to match mine. "You're kidding. They couldn't. They wouldn't. Would they?"

"Who knows?" I stared down at my hands. "Nobody knows what would happen to the fountain, if they did. The new commissioner won't give a straight answer. People are pissed. But Foxwoods - well, apparently, they're all for it."

"Of course," he said, bitterly. The development was half-finished when he moved away, but Cole still felt the same knee-jerk reaction that everyone from Alki did when they thought about Foxwoods. I could remember the protest signs when the developers first talked about building it. SAVE OUR COMMUNITY! SAY NO TO FOXWOODS!

"But, who knows," I said, leaning forward to switch off the T.V. before the static actually bored a hole in my eardrums. "Maybe it'll all come to nothing."

Something told me it wouldn't, but I didn't want to have this discussion with Cole anymore. I liked it better when he was smiling.

"So, what's new with you?" I turned to him, smiling, trying hard to keep my tone casual and light.

He shook his head a little. "Nothing," he said. "I mean, nothing's ever new. But I guess it's all new to you." He paused, gathering his thoughts. "It's just been a string of odd jobs and boring shithole towns since I left. I dunno what I thought I'd find out there, but it wasn't much."

This was a mistake. Thinking about him leaving - it still hurt like a gaping hole in my chest, just like it had happened yesterday. What a ridiculous sap I was.

Get over it, Heather. Almost ten years ago. You really still pining for this asshole?

"I could've told you that," I said, as cheerily as I could manage. "But sometimes people just need a fresh start, I guess."

"Mhmm." He picked up the remote and turned it around, absently, in his hands. "Yeah, you know - not much to tell. But you're working down at Joe's now, huh?"

Instantly, the memory of his smell came back. "How'd you know?" I asked, a little more sharply than I meant to.

He raised an eyebrow. "You smell like tires," he said, with a halfway grin. "Sorry - but it's true."

I laughed a little, but I couldn't shake the feeling. *You saw me there. You were watching me. I didn't see you, but I smelled you. It might reek like rubber and automotive oil in that place, but it wasn't strong enough to fool my nose.*

"Thanks, dick," I said, thwacking him on the arm. He pouted a little, and I pretended like it hadn't been an excuse to touch him. "Maybe it's time for a shower." I made a move to stand up.

"Nah, no, don't - please, I was just messing with you." His hand shot out and clamped over my arm, holding me in place.

"You mean I don't smell like tires?"

"You absolutely do," he said, his eyes sparkling. "But I like it."

Swallowing hard, I jostled my arm a little. He was still holding on, but he didn't seem too inclined to let go.

Finally, he cleared his throat and sat back, letting me go. It was like he'd just realized what he was doing. After all this time, I couldn't believe how easy it was to slip right back into flirting with him. But I had to put a stop to it.

"It sure beats smelling like fry oil," I said. "And those were basically my only two options. So, you know. I learned a thing or two about lug nuts, and now I answer Jim's phones. There are definitely worse jobs out there."

"Absolutely," he said. "You don't happen to know if he's hiring, do you?" There was that sparkle again. Was he joking?

"Doubt it," I said. I couldn't imagine working in close quarters with Cole. I'd go insane. "Besides, you have to be certified. Occasionally changing a tire doesn't count."

"Hey," said Cole, stretching his legs out in front of him, and interlacing his hands behind his head. "For all you know, I went to trade school while I was away."

"But you didn't," I said. "Did you?"

"Nah." He leaned his head back. "But I always felt like I'd make a good mechanic."

"Well, rebuilding an engine requires something more than 'feelings,' I think." I wrapped my arms around myself, suddenly chilled. "But I'm sure you can find work around here. Even if it does involve fry oil."

"Those sound like tomorrow's worries," he said. "For now, I'm just glad to be back."

I was afraid to ask him how long he was planning to stay. I was afraid to ask him much of anything. Especially the questions I most wanted the answers to.

"Tomorrow's worries," I repeated. "Your grandma used to say that, didn't she?"

"She sure did." He smiled, wistfully. "That, and - 'you'll

always regret the things you didn't do, more than the things you did.'"

"I'm not sure I believe that one," I said. "As much as I hate to contradict her."

He looked at me. "My grandma was always right," he said, firmly. "And she was right about that, too."

So you don't regret leaving.

I didn't dare ask. I couldn't afford to seem like I still cared.

"It's hard to believe that applies to you at all," I said, leaning back on the sofa. "Seems like you always did exactly what you wanted."

"No," he said, still looking at me. My throat went a little dry. "Not always. Not even half the time."

Forcing a laugh, I let my eyes drift over to him again. "So, *this* is Cole Jackman reigning in his impulses? Holy shit. I don't want to know what the real you is like."

"Trust me," he said, his voice suddenly a low growl that made goosebumps rise all over my body. "You really don't."

I laughed again, loudly, to dispel the tension in the air. But he was still looking at me, with a stare even more intense than usual. I shivered, rubbing my hands up and down my arms. "Little chilly in here, isn't it?" I said, not really expecting an answer.

"Go on," he said, his voice still low. "Ask me what I regret. I can tell you want to."

Shrugging uncomfortably, I drew my legs up to the sofa and folded them under me. "You obviously want to tell me," I said. "So do I need to ask?"

"Yeah," he said, nodding slowly. "You need to ask."

I licked my lips. In the corner, a very old wall clock ticked loudly. It was just out of reach, above the kitchen counter - impossible for me to get to, without climbing up on said counter, which was always cluttered with too many appliances that I never used. So the clock stayed, annoying ticking sound and all, while I waited for the battery to die.

I'd been waiting for an awfully long time now.

The air was thick with anticipation. I understood implicitly what he meant. If I asked, that was permission. Permission to stop pretending we didn't want each other. To my humiliation, I realized that my eyes must have been filled with longing. I hadn't hidden my feelings well at all. Stupid me, I'd thought I could do it. But he knew. He always knew.

His eyes, on the other hand, were just *hungry*.

But he wasn't going to give in. Not unless I wanted him to.

"Do you regret leaving?"

It was a compromise. Not the question he wanted me to ask, but I wasn't going to keep pretending.

Cole let out a small, frustrated sigh. "Yes," he said. "But not half as much as I regret that day we met up behind the school after fifth period."

He said: "Do you remember?"

I did.

The feeling of the late summer sun on my skin, Cole in his hand-me-down Nirvana shirt and camo pants. Even back then, he had that persistent stubble, shadowing his face. Everybody else left when the bell rang, but we didn't.

"I should've kissed you then," he said, his voice barely above a murmur. "I don't know why I didn't."

My hands were clenched tightly in my lap. I couldn't look at him. "Cause you knew better," I said.

"Nah." He'd slid closer, somehow, without me noticing. But I noticed now. I could feel the heat of his body. "Something tells me that's not why."

I looked up, finally. His tongue flicked out to moisten his lips, and he smiled.

This was my last chance to reclaim my sanity.

Come on, grown-up-Heather. The train is leaving the station. You better push him away now. Otherwise…

I kissed him.

With a soft growl, he leaned into it, curling his tongue into my half-open mouth. His hand splayed on the side of my neck, holding me in place - as if I would go anywhere. As if I *could*.

I rose up, lifting my knee over his lap and straddling him as we parted briefly for air. He grasped my hips and stood, carrying me with my legs wrapped around his waist, until we reached my bed. He dropped me there gently, laughing a little, and crawled on top of me, to begin methodically stripping off the clothes I'd put on such a short time ago.

I lay still and let him do this, peeling back the layers until I was naked, silently worshipping my oh-so-neglected body with his eyes and his hands. But it wasn't long before I needed to see him too, and I helped him pull off his borrowed shirt and pants so I could admire every angle and plane and taut muscle of the man he'd become.

And that was the moment I lost myself to him, letting his fingers stroke me through bliss, shattering to pieces under his touch. He just smiled for a long time, planting little kisses on my face, until my breathing started to slow down.

"You're so beautiful," he said, with a sense of awe in his voice that I didn't miss. "I could just watch you all night."

I smiled. "I don't remember you being this patient."

"Course I wasn't," he chuckled. "I was eighteen. It's hard to relax and enjoy the scenery when you're sporting a hard-on 24/7."

Giggling, I lifted myself up on my elbow. "I feel like I would've remembered that."

"I got pretty good at hiding it," he said. "Until you didn't want me to."

Remember our first time?

I blinked. He must have spoken out loud, because I heard his voice, but at the same time, it seemed like it was coming out of my own head. I must be more delirious from my orgasm than I thought.

But of course, I remembered. It was sweaty and awkward and passionate and perfect, just like everyone's first time should be. He hated hurting me, but I urged him on, loving the warm glow that came from us being connected so intimately.

It was a different kind of pleasure for me, no toe-curling climax, just a feeling of *rightness* and the sense that he was meant to fill me up like that. He was always very concerned that I couldn't come that way, but I never cared. It wasn't like he didn't find other ways to pleasure me.

Cole's hand slid partially under my neck, cupping me possessively, his thumb stroking my pulse point as he kissed me, long and slow. He pressed his body up against me, letting his hardness nudge at my still-sensitive entrance. I moaned into his mouth and tried to hook my leg over his hip, but he stilled me with his hand, sliding it down from my neck to my thigh.

"Not yet," he murmured, when he broke away for air. "I want to try something else with you. I've been thinking about it for ten years."

I had to giggle again, to hide the shiver that went through me. "You're ridiculous," I said. But I didn't protest when he got to his feet and grabbed my hand, pulling me up. I looked at him curiously, his wicked smile making me throb for his touch all over again.

He pointed at the full-length mirror next to my dresser. "Anybody ever fuck you in front of that?" His voice rumbled low and enticing, and there was only the slightest hint of jealousy in his question. Just enough to make my heart twinge.

No, never. Nobody's fucked me anywhere. Not since you.

I'd had *encounters*, of course, but they never went that far. Guys never seemed to mind where they got their rocks off, as long as they did it somewhere. I always meant to let it happen, to let some other man wipe the memory of Cole from my body, but I never could. When the time came, it always felt wrong.

And now, I was finally going to let it happen - with the one guy I'd never wanted to see again.

"No," I said, finally.

"I'm going to," he murmured, pressing up against my back, circling his arms around me from behind. His cock pulsed against my lower back, a searing heat on my skin. "I'm going to look into your eyes while you watch me fucking you. I'm going to *see* my cock sliding into your pussy. I'll be able to see every part of your body reacting to me, and you won't be able to hide anything. How does that sound, Sunshine?"

I was hot all over, my face burning, my body shuddering at the image in my mind. He never talked like that when we were teenagers. *Nobody* had ever talked to me like that.

Sunshine. That was the name he'd used for me back when we were just stupid, crazy kids in love. I remembered it very well - the conversation we had, where I complained that there are no good nicknames for Heather. He ran through a ridiculous list of things he might call me, and finally settled on Sunshine. When I pointed out that it wasn't any shorter than Heather, he just laughed and kissed the tip of my nose.

He was a different man now. He was a *man*, period. And I'd never felt more like a woman than I did in that moment, feeling him breathe against me while he waited for an answer.

"That sounds good," I whispered, punctuating with a gasp when I felt the heavy twitch against my back. Just my response was enough to make him even harder.

He pulled back a little, laying his hands on my shoulders and steering me over to the mirror. I looked into his eyes for as long as I could stand it, letting their fierce blue glint penetrate everything I'd tried to hide from him. All the feelings I wanted to deny. The longing I still felt for him, every day.

My own reflection was hardly recognizable. My hair was wild, my lips swollen and parted to allow for each heavy breath. As my chest rose and fell, it was impossible not to notice how stiff my nipples had grown.

Cole lifted each of my hands, planting them firmly on the wall on either side of the mirror.

"Step back." He gripped my hips, firmly, pulling me towards him. "Step back and spread your legs for me, baby."

I was completely under his spell, following his orders, curving my back and presenting myself to him. He made a low noise of appreciation, stroking one hip lightly when I was right where he wanted me.

"Perfect," he whispered, his blunt hardness pressing urgently, breaching me open, stretching and sliding in endlessly. I let out a ragged moan, my lower back curving even more sharply to meet him, inviting him in deep enough to nudge my core. An intense shiver of pleasure mingled with pain, and I clutched hard at the wall.

"You're so tight," he panted in my ear, as I felt him stiffen and swell inside me. "It's been a while, hasn't it?"

I let out a huff of laughter. "You have no idea how long," I whispered, raising my head to look at him in the mirror. His eyes were dark and feral, and somehow that made me want him even more.

His hand snaked around my chest, lightly stroking each nipple with the side of his thumb, just enough to make me shiver. Then, he slid down my stomach, his hand stopping just above where we were joined.

"Look." His teeth scraped against my earlobe. "Look at us, Sunshine."

I looked.

It was beautifully obscene. I had to drag my eyes back up to my own face, and higher, to his, looming over my shoulder, to convince myself it was real. It was really us, our bodies, our fucking *souls* -

No. No. *No.* I couldn't let this become more than it was. A purely physical encounter, getting ten years' worth of pent-up desires out of our systems.

I wasn't fooling anyone, least of all myself.

As he moved inside of me, one arm holding me steady, he slid his other hand along my shoulder, up my arm, until his hand covered mine against the wall. Slowly, he interlaced his fingers with mine.

I couldn't look at him anymore. Letting my neck go loose, I closed my eyes, resting my forehead against the cool glass.

Cole let out a low growl. The hand that was resting on my stomach shot upwards, grabbing my chin and lifting my head up.

"Look at me." His grip was firm, but not quite enough to hurt. I let my eyes flick up to his briefly, but it was too much. Too much, too soon, after nine and a half years of nothing but memories. Nine and half years of trying to forget.

He let go of my chin a moment later and slid his hand back down the front of my body, stopping where we were joined, pressing his fingers gently against my over-sensitized flesh. I hissed, rocking forward, feeling the protesting tug of his hardness inside me as I did. I rocked backwards to accommodate it, and he rewarded me with a firm finger circling my clit.

Eyes hazy, heartbeat thudding in my ears, I stared at him in the mirror. Before, I couldn't look. Now, I couldn't look away. His face showed everything. He was captivated, enraptured, losing himself in me, but with a hard edge of hunger and the desire to possess. I had never seen this side of him before. I'd never known that I *wanted* to.

"Take it, baby," he panted in my ear, his thrusts growing faster, more erratic. "Take it. *You're mine.*"

I exploded. Crying out wordlessly as my body snapped to a taut bow and then sagged, I tried to hold myself upright. Without Cole's strong arm around me, I would have failed. Shuddering pleasure overtook me. When I was able to raise my head again, trembling all over, I realized Cole wasn't finished. His cock still twitched and throbbed inside me, and his jaw was clenched with the effort of holding back.

"You ready?" he whispered.

I wanted to say something cheeky. What if I wasn't? He clearly couldn't hold out for much longer.

But all I did was nod, weakly.

"Tell me you want it," he growled. "Tell me."

I swallowed thickly. "I want it."

"Tell me you've been thinking about it since the day we met." His voice was dark and commanding. The instant he said it, it became true - and I couldn't remember if it was before or not. It didn't matter. It was true now.

"I have," I whispered.

He nibbled at the back of my neck, his arm holding me steady for a few more shallow thrusts. He halted deep inside me. A soft noise escaped from the back of his throat.

"Tell...me..." he breathed, and I could feel every muscle of his body clenching, on the verge of climax. "Tell me what you want. Say the words."

"I want...I need..." My breath came out in sobs. "I *need* you to come inside me."

He growled, his eyes going hazy, hips jerking a frantic rhythm as he spilled deep inside me, just like I'd wanted. Little shudders of pleasure went through me, almost as if I was feeling tiny aftershocks of his climax.

I sagged, exhausted, relying even more on his grip to hold me, but I could feel his muscles start to tremble. Neither of us moved for a few moments, breathing harshly, still connected in the most intimate possible way.

Finally, he slipped out of me and stepped back, giving me some room to right myself. The mirror was fogged with our breath, and I couldn't see my face. That was probably just as well.

Exhaustion crept in, and my eyelids were so heavy I almost didn't bother going into the bathroom to clean up. But I couldn't abide sticky sheets, so I managed - only just, before stumbling into bed and crawling under the covers. Cole was already there, his eyes closed, and it seemed so right I didn't even question it.

"Missed you, Sunshine," he mumbled, as I slung my arm around his torso.

"Mhmm," I managed to respond, before sleep took over.

Chapter Three

When I woke up in the morning, Cole was gone.

I don't know why that surprised me. At first, I really considered that I might have dreamed it all. But then my eyes drifted to his borrowed clothes, still lying in a lump at the foot of my bed. And my body slowly became aware of the ache between my legs, and the twinge of pain in my lower back, and there was really no doubt.

He's gone.

Disappointment coursed through my veins like poison. Did he just come back to convince himself he could still have me? Did he get off on the knowledge that I was wrapped so tightly around his little finger, even after all these years? I didn't resist him, not even for a moment. When he looked at me with those *fuck-me* eyes, it was like I became a different person.

A much less sensible person.

As I walked to the bathroom, something caught the corner of my eye. It looked like there was something on the fridge - something that didn't belong.

A piece of paper, maybe.

A note.

I forced myself not to run and look. I washed my face, brushed my teeth, and stared at myself in the mirror until my heart stopped pounding.

I don't care. I don't care. I really, really don't care.

Finally, I walked out to the kitchen.

It was a note, written on the back of a pizza coupon flyer. I recognized Cole's handwriting immediately. It was somehow both swooping and jagged, just like it had been in high school.

Heather,

Sorry, I didn't want to wake you. Thanks for everything. I'd love to go for a hike today and catch up some more, if you're not busy. Call me.

His phone number was scrawled at the bottom, and he hadn't bothered to sign it. It was characteristically terse, though I couldn't figure out what else I was expecting. *Dear Heather, thanks for letting me fuck you in front of a mirror while we stared into each other's eyes like two lovelorn teenagers. Had a great time. I know I can't stay with you any more since you refuse to tell Steve and Andrea that you've succumbed to my charms once again, but I sure would love to fuck you in the woods later…*

Once upon a time, when were young, that was all "hiking" meant. We'd go just far enough to be isolated, and retreat somewhere under a covering of branches, somewhere only the birds and the crickets could hear us. Hiking was practically the official pastime of the Pacific Northwest, so it was the perfect excuse. Though if our parents didn't at least have an inkling of what was really happening, well - I'd be shocked.

Maybe that's not what he meant.

Yeah, and maybe I'd win the lottery tomorrow. Anything was possible.

I sat with the phone in my hand for twenty minutes, trying to figure out what I could say. I wanted to hear his voice again, wanted it desperately, but at the same time I very much *didn't*.

Finally, I typed out a text message instead. It was a compromise. For whom, I didn't know.

Where?

The answer came less than a minute later.

You know where.

An irrational stab of anger went through my chest. I hated that the fountain was no longer mine. I'd never be able to go there again without thinking of him, and that was the absolute last thing I needed. This whole place was already stained with memories of him. Even my apartment, now, would never be the same.

But that was my fault, just as much as his. It was just easier to blame somebody else.

I wasn't hungry, but I ate a few handfuls of granola and grabbed a water bottle before I headed out to the fountain.

The ground was still spongey from the rain, but today there was nothing but sunshine and chirping birds. The weather made about as much sense as my feelings for Cole. It was much easier to stay angry and aloof when he wasn't right in front of me, fixing me with those piercing blue eyes that made me forget all the very good reasons why I didn't want him in my life again.

Suddenly, I caught his scent in the air. Memories of last night came back in a rush, sending a flare of heat between my legs and making my knees weaken slightly.

You're mine.

I shook my head, sending the images scattering. He didn't mean it. Obviously, it was just one of those things you say in the heat of the moment. And my body's *completely* irrational reaction wasn't even worth worrying about. Just because there was a primal appeal to the idea of being owned by an alpha male who growled in your ear while he fucked you in front of a mirror…

Well, that was no reason to act like an idiot.

Maybe it was too late for that.

This time, I saw him before he saw me. He was standing by the fountain, his hands shoved deep in his pockets, wearing a flannel shirt with the sleeves rolled up to his elbows.

"Take a picture," he said, without turning around. "It'll last longer."

I walked up to him, stopping a few feet away, keeping my eyes on the fountain. "Good morning to you too," I said.

"Heather." He cleared his throat. "Hey. Look at me for a second."

He was smiling, but subdued, and I held my breath. The last thing I wanted right now was to have some kind of serious discussion about…anything, really. Especially not whatever was happening between us.

"I didn't mean for things to move so fast," he said. "I mean - last night, it was amazing, but that wasn't how I planned it. I just wanted to see you again. Talk to you. Apologize, maybe, if it's not too late for that."

"A little bit," I said, lightly. "But it doesn't matter. Not anymore. It's been so long, we're both different people now."

"Right," he said, not sounding completely convinced. "Well, I'm sorry anyway."

I shrugged. "Water under the bridge."

Cole chuckled a little. "Remember when we used to play poker after school, with Josh and Lisa and everybody else?"

"Yeah," I said. "I remember when Principal Bouchard busted us for gambling on school property. But you convinced him to let us keep playing, as long as we gambled with candy we bought out of the school vending machine, instead of quarters."

"One of my finest hours," Cole agreed. "But my point is, you had a terrible poker face back then. And you still do."

I felt the back of my neck flush hot. "Don't know what you're talking about," I said.

"Sure." Cole glanced at me, sidelong. "I just want you to know, I don't blame you for being mad. Even if you're not mad. I understand why you would be. I never should have left the way I did, even if we weren't dating anymore. It wasn't fair to you."

I'd been waiting to hear that for so long. But now, standing in front of the fountain, I just couldn't hear it.

"Thank you," I said. "So are we going to go on that hike, or what?"

We started walking in silence, as the sun rose higher in the sky. It didn't take long for Cole to start talking, asking me idle questions about what had happened in Douglas Mountain since he left. Foxwoods made him grimace, but when I told him that good old Arthur Craven had become their community board leader, he couldn't stop laughing.

"I can't imagine a more perfect job for him," Cole said, grinning, as he stripped off his flannel shirt and tied it around his waist. His skin glistened in the sunlight, and I forced myself to look away. "Please tell me that he's still sending regular bulletins to the police about suspicious persons."

"He once spent every afternoon, for a solid week, photographing all the cars that he thought were speeding through the side-streets. He brought them all down to the station in a big manila envelope, and he couldn't understand why they didn't consider his blurry cell phone pictures actionable."

"That's the most beautiful thing I've ever heard," he said. "How about the letters to the editor?"

"Every week, like clockwork."

"Guess some things never change." Cole stopped, suddenly, his head jerking upwards and his eyes narrowing slightly.

"Are you okay?" I asked.

He held his finger to his lips. I kept still for a long moment, straining my ears for whatever he'd heard.

And then I noticed it. A soft rustling. I was being followed, once again.

"It's just…" I drifted off when Cole looked at me, sharply.

"Do you hear that?" he whispered, his whole body tensing.

"Yeah, I was just going to say, it's the…"

The noise grew louder, and all of a sudden, a cougar stepped out into our path.

I swallowed hard. They were almost never this brazen.

Unless they've already made up their mind to attack.

"It's all right," I said, softly. The huge animal just stared. I could feel the tension in Cole's body like it was my own, my muscles stiffening, my jaw clenching. "He doesn't want to hurt anybody."

I didn't know that. I couldn't. This felt different from every other encounter. Cole was there, and Cole was not welcome. I got that message, loud and clear, just as if the cougar had told me in so many words.

The cougar crouched low, his ears flattening back against his head. My heart constricted with a sudden fear. I had never seen that posture before, but I knew what it meant.

I stared at the animal, but he wasn't interested in me. For once, he was captivated by someone else. And Cole was staring back. But the cougar didn't back down. He crept forward, his tail twitching back and forth rapidly, and I resolved to do something drastic. Never taking my eyes off the cougar, I crouched down and picked up a rock. Hefting it carefully, judging the distance I'd need, I whispered to Cole.

"I'm going to try and hit him. If I can startle him enough, he'll run away."

There was a moment of silence from Cole, which felt like years.

"No," he said, finally, his voice low and rough. "He won't."

What the fuck do you know?

I hauled back, and threw. I'd been aiming for his head, but I went a little wide and hit his shoulder. The cougar hardly flinched. He just kept staring, his back legs pumping up and down slightly. Readying his pounce.

My heart was throbbing, every muscle and bone in my body starting to ache. A sharp pain, starting at my fingertips, rapidly crawled its way up my arms.

Cole's voice sounded rougher than ever.

"Run."

I choked, tripping forward onto the ground. I didn't know what was happening. I couldn't even see the cougar anymore, or anything at all. My vision filled with red. Agony tore through my body, and I screamed, writhing on the dirt. When it had faded enough for me to look up, trying to blink away the creeping blackness at the corners of my eyes, I saw it.

I saw something impossible.

Cole was not Cole. In his place, there stood a massive beast covered with long black fur. But I *understood* it was him, the same way you always know who someone is supposed to be in a dream, even when they wear someone else's face. The eyes were bright blue, the muzzle long, the ears tall and pointed - a wolf. Just not like any wolf I'd ever seen.

He was still semi-upright, but he pitched forward on all fours as I watched. Growling. He was still staring at the cougar, who had now backed several steps away. The tail still twitched, but he was confused now. A little frightened. Cole crouched down low on the ground, baring his teeth.

With one massive leap forward, the cougar swatted at his face. Cole dodged so quickly he became a blur, jumping on top of the cougar and grabbing the loose skin on the back of its neck in his teeth. I'd never heard the unholy yowl of a big frightened cat before, and I hoped I never would again. Cole jerked his head from side to side, shaking the cougar like a rag doll. When he finally let go, the tawny animal turned tail and fled deep into the forest.

I was panting. My heart pounded insistently against my ribs. My fingers were buried in the dirt, gripping for dear life, and the adrenaline still coursed through my veins.

What the fuck, Cole? I wanted to shout. But I had no voice. No breath. I sucked in oxygen and forced myself to breathe it out, over and over again, while black spots swam in front of my eyes.

Cole, the wolf, turned to me. He shook his head, and the transformation started. Once again, a deep ache settled in my bones, but this was calmer, more bearable. I gritted my teeth as I watched him shift back into the form that I knew. The ache disappeared. Well - not all of it. One ache remained, of a slightly different nature than all the others. An irrational hunger, demanding satisfaction.

He was breathing hard. His chest glistened with sweat, his hair flopping down over one eye, and his jeans had ripped down the sides from the sudden appearance of his wolf flanks. But it was the bulge between his legs that I couldn't stop staring at. Whatever this insane urge was, he felt it too.

I wanted answers. I needed answers. I needed to know what the hell was going on, what the hell he *was* - but I didn't need any of that as much as I needed him inside me.

Now. Immediately. Right here, in the middle of the forest, on the dirt.

There was no need to say a single word about it. We were of one mind, crashing together on the ground, his bulk pinning me down to the earth. He yanked my shorts down and scrambled to unzip what was left of his jeans, while I lifted my hips towards him, the urge to feel him already starting to drive me insane.

He was harder than I'd ever seen him before, his cock angry

and throbbing, but I only had a moment to appreciate it before he slammed inside me.

My head jerked back, an inhuman noise coming from the back of my throat. Grabbing fistfuls of dried leaves, I tried to keep it together, tried to keep myself from shattering into a thousand pieces, tried to stop myself from screaming so loud that Arthur Craven would call the cops. But I couldn't. I didn't. My legs curled around Cole's waist, urging him faster, harder, deeper. I wasn't sure I could take any more, but I wanted to find out.

My climax hit me like a freight train. If I'd been capable of thinking, I would have expected it to wane as suddenly as it peaked. But it didn't. I kept on shuddering, moaning, my hips bucking up and down as Cole fucked me through it. Finally his body couldn't resist the tight clench of my inner muscles, and he groaned, his eyes closing for a moment as he came deep inside me.

I didn't even have the time to breathe, to tell myself I wasn't disappointed, even though the remainders of my climax still quivered in my core - before he started thrusting again, stoking the fire. I moaned again, staring into his eyes as he pushed his own seed deeper inside me. At first, I saw the slight wince on his face, as his over-sensitized cockhead rubbed against my tight walls. But a moment later he exhaled, growing even harder inside me.

Wave after wave of pleasure washed over me, until I hardly recognized by own hoarse cries of ecstasy. Cole thrust harder and faster, his breathing ragged. He was like a man possessed. Even at our most insatiable, our high school trysts had never been like *this*.

I was lost in it, the intensity taking over and blacking out my vision, my thoughts, everything except the feeling of him inside me. Inch by inch, thrust by thrust, we were sliding across the forest floor.

We seemed to go on like this forever, until every muscle in my body ached deliciously from the tension, until my voice disappeared, until I was well past the point of exhaustion, but I couldn't have cared less.

As the sensations finally began to fade, leaving me numb and throbbing, Cole's movements stuttered. He panted my name, his eyes rolling back as he groaned and spilled inside me once more.

I didn't move for a long time, letting my body stay limp and heavy on the ground. It took a long time to catch my breath, and a headache was throbbing to life at the base of my neck.

Worth it.

Laughing weakly at myself, I heard Cole make a small noise. I opened my eyes. He was still on top of me, resting on his forearms, wearing a halfway grin that made my heart ache almost as much as my head.

"Well," he said, as a bead of sweat dripped off the ends of his hair and landed on my chest.

"Yeah," I said. More eloquent words failed me, and Cole hauled himself to his feet with a monumental effort. He took a long swig from my water bottle, then handed it to me.

I sat up, staring at him. All the shock and confusion and unanswered questions were coming back in a tidal wave, and he must have seen it on my face, because he spoke up before I could.

"I can explain," he said. "But, uh, maybe we should go get cleaned up first."

"No," I said, screwing the lid back on my water and plopping it down on the dirt beside me. "Go ahead and explain now."

He cleared his throat, shuffling his feet slightly. "Can I at least go somewhere and put some pants on? I'll feel genuinely bad if some unsuspecting family comes hiking by."

"Fine," I said, struggling to my feet. "We can walk and talk." I grabbed my clothes and pulled them on again, as best I could.

Carrying the shreds of his ruined jeans over one arm, Cole

started up the path, occasionally glancing around him, like he was ready to disappear into the underbrush at the slightest sign of life nearby.

"So, what you just saw back there," he began. "It's kind of - it's kind of an open secret around here."

"What, that you're a werewolf?" The whole thing was so absurd that I couldn't even laugh at it.

He snorted. "I appreciate you taking it in stride, but no, not exactly. I mean - you could call it that. But there are others, and they don't all turn into wolves."

"Of course not." I blinked a few times, trying to convince myself that I was dreaming. "How could I be so small-minded?"

Steve and Andrea were both at work, thankfully. I didn't have to worry about explaining why I was bringing a naked, dirt-streaked Cole Jackman back to my apartment. He insisted we should both have a shower before he explained any more, and I insisted on the shower being separate. I was almost positive I couldn't handle another round, but if I had a soapy Cole at my disposal my body might end up disagreeing.

"So there's more than one of you," I said, as he toweled off his hair.

"A lot more," he said. "Quite a few of your friends are moonlighting as bears and badgers. Like I said - it's kind of an open secret around here. Our kind sticks together. We're like a family. A clan."

"Sure," I said. It made about as much sense as anything else I'd had to process today. Any minute now, I expected it to really sink in, and I'd start screaming and running around in circles, panicking over my shattered perception of reality.

Cole squinted at me. "Are you sure you're feeling okay?"

I shrugged. "Why? Do people usually react differently?"

"I don't know," he said. "Never told anyone before."

That one threw me for a loop. "Really?" I said. "Never?"

"I mean, when do you bring it up?" he chuckled. "Nah. Never had the opportunity."

"But you…" I gestured vaguely. "It didn't exactly seem like you could help it, when it happened."

"I can't," he said. "Sometimes we can change at will, but there are times when it's involuntary. Every night there's a full moon. Any time we feel we're in danger. And sometimes, just when we're really, really angry…"

"That sounds terrifying," I said, because it really did.

Cole's mouth twisted into something that wasn't really a smile. "You get used to it," he said.

"But you've never done that in front of somebody who wasn't…one of you," I said. "I'm sorry. I don't really, uh…I don't know what you call yourselves."

"We don't have much occasion to call ourselves anything," he said, shrugging. "We're just *us*."

That made so much sense, it almost made my headache worse.

"And no," he went on. "I've never been with somebody when they were suddenly threatened by a wild animal, I guess."

I bristled. "He wasn't a threat. They follow me all the time. If they wanted to hurt me, they've had plenty of opportunities before today." Something occurred to me, suddenly. "Hold up - he wasn't, uh, one of *you guys* - was he?"

"No," said Cole, quickly. "Absolutely not. That's a wild animal, Heather. I know you've got a 'way' with them or whatever, but you really need to be more careful."

"And somehow I've survived the last ten years without you babysitting me," I said, dryly. "Amazing."

He gave me a look. "There's a lot of things you don't know," he said.

Annoyance spiked through my chest. "Wow, you still know how to charm a girl, Jackman." I stood up, tired of listening to his bullshit. "Are we done here?"

He instantly looked ashamed of himself. "Heather, I'm sorry. Come on. Sit down. This is, you know - it's just tough to explain, that's all. I didn't mean to sound like…"

I smiled wryly.

"My dad," I said. "Yeah, you nailed it." I hadn't realized it until he led me there, but my instant *fuck-you* reaction was a sure sign that Cole had suddenly reminded me of my old man.

"It'd be better if I took you to meet our leader," he said. "The Alpha. Well, I mean - you've met her. But you haven't really *met* her."

My brain stuttered. "*Her?*" I repeated.

"Yeah," said Cole, frowning at me. "Why?"

Finally, the hysterical laugh that had been clawing at my brain escaped through my mouth, and I sprawled back on the sofa, howling. Metaphorically speaking, of course.

"I don't know," I gasped, finally. Cole was still frowning. "I don't know. For some reason, I guess I just thought werewolves and werebears and…were-whatevers, would be some kind of old boy's club." Wiping my eyes, I sat forward. "I really…I don't have any fucking idea why. Who is it?"

I knew the answer before he could say anything.

"Adanna," I muttered, mostly to myself. "Who else?"

"Who else indeed," he said. There was a meaning behind it, but I couldn't read his face.

"I have to work tomorrow," I said. "But maybe after?"

"Sure," he said. "I'll talk to her. Let her know what's happened. I think she wants to talk to you anyway, about the fountain and all that."

My head was swimming, but I just nodded and laid back on the sofa. "You have somewhere to stay tonight?"

"Yeah. Down at the motel on Hobart Road." He jerked his thumb in a random direction. "Hasn't changed a bit."

I laughed. "Same TVs, same fridges, same pillowcases - bless 'em."

He paused awkwardly in the hallway, like he couldn't figure out how he was supposed to say goodbye. A kiss? A hug? Another round of bone-crackingly passionate sex?

Yeah, no. That was a bad idea.

I was almost one hundred percent sure.

"See you tomorrow, Heather," he said, finally, his voice very soft. "Thanks for…you know. Not running away screaming."

"I bet you say that to all the girls," I said, staring at the ceiling.

"Nah," he said. "Just you."

A few moments later, I heard the sound of my front door creaking shut.

Chapter Four

"Excuse me?"

A voice roused me out of my distracted musings behind the counter at Joe's Automotive. I felt my lips draw into a thin line. It was Arthur Craven. Of course it was Arthur Craven.

"Hello, Mr. Craven," I said, pasting on a smile. "What can I do for you today?"

He folded his arms across his chest. "I want to know," he said. "I want to know what you people are doing."

I clenched my teeth so hard, I swore they started to disintegrate.

"Joe," I called over my shoulder. "Mr. Craven wants to know what we're doing."

My smile got a little more brittle as I waited, but it stayed put. I turned my attention to shuffling papers on my desk, pretending that I couldn't feel Arthur's eyes boring a hole in me.

Joe emerged, wiping his hands with a greasy rag. "You're going to have to be more specific, Artie."

I looked up, just in time to see Arthur cringe. He'd always been very clear about his desire to be referred to only as Arthur, and Joe had always been very clear that he didn't give a shit. The level of perfectly polite hostility between these two men was an absolute joy to behold.

"Who did the last tune-up on my car?" Arthur demanded, taking a step closer. Joe took a step as well, to meet him. His chest was squared, and I prayed - not for the first time - that they'd actually come to blows. They never did, but a girl can dream.

"I did," said Joe. "You have a problem with my work?"

Arthur paled slightly, but continued. "It's *rattling*," he hissed. "Someone explain to me why my car would be rattling right after you so *happened* to touch it."

"I can think of quite a few reasons." Joe cracked his knuckles. "None of them are my fault, though."

"Well, isn't that convenient," Arthur sneered. "I'm going to get it looked at. Somewhere else. If they tell me differently, you can believe I'll be back - and I'll be calling the Better Business Bureau. And you can kiss goodbye to that five-star Yelp rating." He made a *poof* gesture with his hand. "Gone!"

Joe was already halfway through the connecting doorway. "Have a great afternoon, Artie."

"Oh, my God," I muttered, my head dropping on the desk as soon as the door slammed. I had a low tolerance for Arthur's bullshit on a good day. But now, when I was still trying to wrap my head around the fact that my ex-boyfriend was a werewolf...

Emphasis on the ex part of ex-boyfriend, of course. Even if we *were* fucking on the regular.

God damn it, how did I get myself into this situation?

"Heather, Adanna. Adanna, Heather." Cole cleared his throat. "Sorry, I'm not up on the etiquette for introducing people who've known each other for a decade."

Suddenly, Adanna's secretive smile had taken on a whole new meaning. I shook her hand, trying to wrap my head around everything, and failing miserably.

"Welcome," she said. "There are precious few people who've seen what you have seen, Heather."

I swallowed with an effort. "I understand that. And I appreciate your, um…hospitality." That definitely wasn't the right word, but it was the best one I could think of.

She nodded, making a gracefully dismissive gesture with her hand. "It's bound to happen from time to time, and we try to take it in stride. It's risky, you understand - as much as possible, we try to stay unnoticed by the world at large."

"Of course."

Cole was standing, silently, in the corner. Overall, he had the bearing of someone who was introducing his new girlfriend to a family member that he found mildly frightening.

Not that I was his girlfriend, of course.

Adanna rose and walked around the desk, going to a sleek black filing cabinet in the corner. It was adorned with trailing plants, their tendrils so long they almost reached the floor.

"Cole tells me that you're very concerned about the fountain," she said, removing a file and flipping through it briefly. "The clan will be having a special council meeting very soon to discuss all the issues surrounding the sale of the land. If you like, you're more than welcome to attend as my guest."

"Thank you," I said, glancing at Cole. He remained mostly unreadable. "I'd be honored."

Adanna smiled. "You can say no, if you'd rather not. I won't be offended. But I know that this place means as much to you as it does to anyone else attending that meeting. Sometimes, this clan makes the mistake of thinking they're the only ones whose opinions matter."

I stifled a laugh. "I think a lot of people make that mistake, from time to time."

"True enough." She set the file down on her desk and sat again, leaning back in her leather captain's chair. "Tell me,

Heather, what do you know about the fountain?"

Was I being tested? Her tone was light enough, but there was a certain weight in the way she was looking at me. I had a feeling that my answers mattered, but I wasn't sure why.

"The same as anybody else around here, I guess." My right eyebrow ticked up, slightly, without my permission. "Unless you all know something that the rest of us don't."

Adanna's smile grew. "Heather, exactly how many of *your* kind do you think live here?"

Feeling stupid, I clasped my hands in my lap. "Uh, well, I guess I don't know."

"Most commonfolk won't live around us for long," she said, her smile growing more gentle. "They grow uncomfortable. They feel that they don't belong. But you're different than most, aren't you?"

I had a feeling I was supposed to nod.

Adanna went on. "Always a misfit? Never really understanding where you fit in with your peers?"

Well, that was true enough. I nodded again.

"You're not one of our bloodline," she said. "But you *are* one of our kin. Your mind and your body know it, even if your brain didn't. It's an old concept, very old - as old as the faiths that our people founded, the ones that worshipped the rocks and the trees and the phases of the moon. Most commonfolk mistrusted us, but some didn't. We called them kin. But of course, that was before the wars."

She sighed, her expression going dark for a moment.

"But," she said, forcing a smile again, "the point is, Heather - you're the only one still here. Everyone you know in Douglas Mountain is one of us."

It should have been a shock. By all rights, I should have fainted right there on her luxurious gray carpet. But I just let it sink in, and found that I wasn't surprised. The explanation made so much *sense*, in a way that completely redefined what the word "sense" even meant.

"I see," I said at last, carefully. Every single one of them. Even Steve and Andrea. By all rights, my head should have been spinning by now - but maybe I'd just maxed out on bizarre knowledge to the point where my brain had no choice to accept it. Maybe later tonight, I'd wake up screaming.

"So," Adanna said, glancing down at the folder again. "The fountain - what do you know?"

"Um." I looked down at my hands. "It's really more about what I *don't* know. Nobody knows who built it, or where the water comes from, or why it's here. That's pretty much all I've got."

"Thank you," she said, closing the folder. "But I'm not interested in what you've been told about the fountain. I want you to tell me what *you* know about it."

I'd never had to put my experiences with the fountain into words before. But something about Adanna's face told me that nothing I'd say would surprise her.

"It's…." I hesitated. "It's…different, isn't it? There's something special about that fountain." I looked up at her, but she just smiled, her eyebrows slightly raised.

"Go on," she said. "This isn't a test. There's no wrong answer."

"It feels peaceful," I said. "But exciting, at the same time. Like anything could happen. And whatever it is, you're going to be okay."

She was nodding. "Have you ever lost time?"

I thought about seeing the sunset, right after I'd left work.

"Yeah," I said. "I guess."

"Has anything else happened at the fountain that you can't explain?"

Yeah. My werewolf ex-boyfriend walking back into my life after nine and a half years of pretending like I didn't exist. And me deciding it would be a good time to take him home and fuck his brains out.

"No," I said. "At least...I don't think so."

"Thank you, Heather." Adanna closed her notebook. "I don't have any answers about the fountain. None of us do. We're trying to understand it, just the same as you. But whatever it is, we know it's important to protect it. This clan's been protecting it for generations. Or maybe it's been protecting us."

I cleared my throat. "I don't think I understand," I admitted.

"Neither do I," she said. "But not everything important has to be understood."

I couldn't tell if that was profound, or just very confusing.

Cole and I left shortly after that, since Adanna had a lot of work to do. All in all, it was a drier meeting than I'd been expecting. For some reason I thought she'd show me her animal form; looking back, it seemed absurd. Like she'd do it for me, as if it was some kind of parlor trick.

"Have *you* ever lost time at the fountain?" I asked Cole, as we walked back towards my place, by some kind of silent agreement.

He nodded. "Most of us have. We were never sure if it was just us, you know, because - well, losing time isn't exactly a foreign experience for us." He half-smiled, a little ruefully. "So it's interesting that you've felt it, too."

Much like everything else I'd been digesting over the last few days, the strange time loss wasn't bothering me as much as it should have. It was simply a thing that happened. I was fine, I felt fine, I didn't see any orbs or rods or wake up with probes in places they shouldn't be.

But still - how strange.

"I must have like...gone catatonic, or something," I said. "I don't know. It's weird."

Thinking about it like that, it should have given me chills. But I felt calm. In a way, I felt like everything I was experiencing now was meant to happen, somehow. Like it was all part of some big, interconnected galactic puzzle. Me and Cole were just two tiny threads in a massive tapestry. Hardly visible, but still a part of the design. And if you tugged too hard, everything would unravel.

That doesn't make any sense. But then again, none of this does.

"Every time I think about the fountain, I feel like I should be afraid of it." Cole kicked a rock fragment with his toe, and it went skittering across the pine needles. "But I never am. When I go there, it feels right. *Everything* feels right."

"I know what you mean."

We were supposed to meet there. The fountain helped me forget all the bitterness, and let go of my anger, so that we could be together.

I almost snorted out loud. That was easily the stupidest thought that had ever crossed my mind.

Thanks, high school Heather.

Whatever, bitch. You know I'm right.

When we got to my front door, Cole hung back, even while I held it open for him.

"You coming in?" I asked, finally.

"Nah," he said, looking regretful. "I have to take care of a few things. But I'll call you tomorrow, okay?"

"Okay," I said.

I wanted to kiss him. God help me, I wanted to kiss Cole Jackman goodnight, like I was his girlfriend or something.

Narrowly, I dodged the temptation.

"Goodnight, Cole."

"Goodnight," he said.

I shut the door before he had a chance to say anything else - with him on the other side of it.

And as I sat there, in the desolate silence of my apartment, I tried to convince myself it was some kind of moral victory.

Chapter Five

My Cole-less evening was spent with the TV droning on in the background, while I flipped through the same shitty coupon magazine five hundred times, not actually *seeing* any of it. Hours passed like this, somehow, until I finally got irritated enough to fling the magazine at the TV, which was currently explaining to me how tires are made.

When I heard someone knocking on my door, my eyes immediately went to the clock.

It's past midnight. What the fuck?

I assumed it must be Cole. But it wasn't like him not to call first, or at least text. Maybe there was something wrong.

Frowning, I hurried to answer it, not bothering to check the peephole.

What I saw on the other side made my jaw drop, and my heart freeze in my chest.

"Hello."

It took me a few seconds to find my voice.

"Dad," I said, numbly, stepping back from the threshold.

He was smiling, a cold and un-comforting smile. But that wasn't unusual for him. I was momentarily taken aback by how much, and how visibly, he'd aged - his hair almost completely gray now, and his face so tired and wan compared to the man I remembered.

"It's good to see you, Heather," he said, making a movement like he was considering a hug - but then wisely pulling back. "How've you been?"

A ridiculous question. But I answered it anyway.

"Good," I said, not even attempting a smile. My face felt completely cold and bloodless; I must be white as a sheet.

"Well, that's good. That's good." He made a few aborted gestures with his hands, looking around the room. "Can I sit down?"

Not waiting for an answer, he went to the sofa and made himself comfortable, plunking his feet on the coffee table, his boots scattering little clumps of dirt all over my old National Geographics. I cringed, but said nothing.

"Listen, before you say anything, I know I should've called." He sighed, as if he was already annoyed at the lecture I wasn't giving him yet. "I know I should've come to visit sooner. But every day goes by, it just gets easier to ignore it - you know?"

He was asking me to take responsibility for my own failure to reach out to him. He didn't want to be the one solely to blame. I just nodded, and sat down gingerly on the other end of the sofa.

"I never stopped thinking about you, or worrying about you," he said. "I'm glad to hear you're doing well. But there's a lot of things changing right now, Heather - stuff that's going to affect both of our lives. And you'll need to make some decisions. You'll have to step up to the plate. Do you think you can do that for me?"

What the hell is he talking about? Is he dying? Does he need a kidney?

Finally, I found my voice.

"What are you talking about, Dad?"

He cleared his throat. "I heard about what happened," he said. "In the woods."

Instantly, my heart constricted in my chest. I knew what he

was talking about before my brain even processed his words, and a hot flush of embarrassment crept up my chest. I'd thought Cole and I were alone, after he…changed. Otherwise I never would have -

"How?" I whispered. "We were…"

"Don't worry about that," he said, waving his hand dismissively. I was starting to get the sense that maybe he didn't know about what happened afterwards. Maybe he really was just talking about Cole's transformation. Relaxing slightly, but only slightly, I looked at him.

"Is it true, or isn't it?" he asked, planting his feet back on the floor and leaning forward with his elbows on his knees, and his face turned slightly towards me.

"It's true," I said, though he clearly already knew. "Why? What do you know about it?"

My father crossed his arms. "First, tell me what he told you."

"Almost nothing," I said. "Just that he's always been this way. There's other people like him. Around here. They're sort of like his family. But he wouldn't tell me who."

That was all my father needed to know.

He nodded, his face twisted into an expression I couldn't quite read. "And you didn't ask any questions?"

"I asked a few," I said, feeling instantly defensive. "But like I said. He wouldn't tell me much. Why are you asking me about this? How did you know?"

"I told you not to worry about that!" he exclaimed angrily, thumping his fist on his own thigh for emphasis. He calmed down a moment later. "I'm sorry, Heather. This is a lot for you to take in. But you have to trust me when I tell you that there's certain things I can't explain right now. I'm going to try and be as clear as possible. There are a lot of things I should have told you when you were a little girl. But I didn't, so you just have to settle down and listen to me now. Okay?"

I didn't answer, but I didn't need to.

He started speaking again.

"There are creatures like Cole all over the world. They tend to stay in packs. That's their nature. This here is one of the biggest. Or it was, until they split off into Foxwoods and Alki. They don't exactly present a united front, nowadays. But they used to be our biggest enemy."

"I…" Where did I even *start*? "I don't really understand what you mean. Who's 'we?'"

"You and me, Heather," my father said, smiling humorlessly. "You and me. Well - you, me, and your mother, technically. But she's left the life behind now." His face clouded over briefly, but he moved on. "There are others, around the world. A lot fewer of us than there are of them. Around here, there's just our family. We're all that's left of the bloodline in the Pacific Northwest. The rest of them inter-mingled and cross-bred with ordinary people. They've lost everything that makes us different."

I was starting to feel light-headed. "And what is that, exactly?" I asked, my voice sounding even fainter than I felt.

"Well, it started out like anything else," he said. "You want a good warrior, you want someone with the sharpest senses, and the quickest reflexes, and all that. But we're talking about berserkers, here. Ordinary warriors won't cut it."

"Berserkers?" I repeated. "Is that what people like Cole are called?"

He snorted. "'People,' she says. Hon, I know they look like men, and talk like them, but trust me. Berserkers aren't people. Not where it counts."

A hot rush of anger flooded my chest. "I don't understand," I said, struggling to keep my voice calm.

"You will," he said. "Trust me."

I cleared my throat. "But *we're* people?"

"Of course we are!" he exclaimed, half-rising in his chair.

"Why would you even ask me that?"

"I don't know, Dad," I said, with the same forced calm. "This is all new to me. Apparently, some people aren't people because they shapeshift. I have no idea what it is that *we* do."

He shook his head, looking up at the ceiling. "I knew I should've started teaching you this stuff earlier," he said, raking his fingers through his hair. "I wanted to start when you were in grade school, but your mother…" He sighed and looked back down at me. "They don't *just* shapeshift. You don't understand. Of course you don't understand." He sighed again. "Look - one thing at a time, all right? I'm trying to explain how our bloodline started. People were chosen. They were trained. But it wasn't enough. We were losing too many to the berserkers. We couldn't match them. But eventually, we started to realize something.

"As it turned out, the best way to fight the berserkers was to *understand* them. At first, they found out by accident. It just so happened that the only people who could stand up to them, the only ones who stood a chance, were the same ones that wild dogs just ran up to. The same people who could tame a bird just by clicking their tongue. Eventually, we saw the connection. Like all animals, the berserkers were reacting to something they weren't even aware of. Something was making them less hostile, and it wasn't anything they could control. At least, not in their animal forms. They fought less effectively. They were distracted.

"The Order started an organized campaign. Children who were found to have this skill were raised as warriors. They were married to each other, and with each generation, their abilities grew stronger. Some of them even seemed to be able to communicate telepathically with animals. There are legends of warriors who used wild animals as their spies."

My mind was somersaulting, trying to take all of this in. "So they're…" I hesitated. "…on *our* side?"

I didn't know which "side" I was really on, or if I even wanted there to be a side. Or even necessarily if this was really happening. Hopefully, I'd wake up from a fever dream in a few hours and forget all of this insanity.

But in the meantime, it seemed best to play along.

"The animals?" My father shrugged. "Who knows? These are all old stories. I don't believe half of them, myself. But there's always a foundation of truth to them."

I clasped my hands tightly in my lap. So I was the product of thousands of years to selective breeding - children taken from their parents and trained to fight people like Cole. Did they even *want* that life? Did they ever have a chance to know anything else?

"The point is," my father went on, "eventually things went too far. Some of the warriors got too close. They started to develop compassionate feelings towards the berserkers, and they believed the berserkers felt the same way towards them. Before long, we had our very own Romeo and Juliet." He smirked. I hated how he kept saying *we*, like he'd even been alive when it happened. He did the same thing when he talked about the Seahawks, but this was a thousand times worse.

"As you might imagine, it was a shit-show." He was still smirking. "Without going into the whole thing, eventually there was a truce. But we kept the bloodline going. We had to. The berserkers sure weren't going to just disappear, so neither were we. Even if the war didn't continue for another hundred years, or another thousand, it didn't matter. We'd be ready."

My knuckles were turning white. "But how did the fighting *start*?"

"Because they're bloodthirsty." His voice was suddenly cold. "They're vermin. All they do is consume and destroy. Someone had to stop them."

Sickness churned in my stomach. I was trying to reconcile this notion with what I knew of Cole, of all the people in his 'pack' -

whoever they might be. Was I the only person in Alki Valley that wasn't a…berserker?

"I still don't understand," I said, fighting to keep my voice calm. "If all this is true, why did you never tell me before? Why are you only coming back now?"

What do you want me to do?

But I was afraid to ask that question. Terrified of what the answer would be.

My father's face grew very serious, all signs of even the bitterest humor gone.

"This is it, Heather," he said. "This is the time. Every year, they get weaker from infighting. Now this whole thing with the fountain - I don't even know if they still remember us, but if they do, they sure aren't thinking about us now. It'll be the last thing they expect. Especially from someone like you."

I couldn't hold the question back any longer.

"The time to do what?"

A hollow smile crept across his face. "Heather," he said, in a tone that was probably meant to be soothing. "Heather, calm down. I'm just asking you to take a stand. It's not going to escalate. If things go well, there won't be any violence at all. I just want you to remind them that we're still here. I want them to remember that they need to uphold their end of the bargain."

"What bargain?" I gnawed on my lower lip, feeling more confused and lightheaded with each passing moment.

My father shook his head. "Right. The treaty. I never explained it. It's simple enough. They have their land, we have ours. It's been in effect for centuries. But over the years, they've pushed the line. Further and further, all over the world, all the clans have started expanding. Every generation cares less about the rules of the one that came before. By now, who knows if they're even teaching their young about it? They've started creeping away from their ancestral lands. Foxwoods, by all rights, is ours. They shouldn't be there. I'm ashamed to say that I ignored it when it happened. I had other things on my mind."

Yes, I remembered. They broke ground on Foxwoods the same day my mother packed her suitcase and threw it in the back of a taxi. I didn't even know taxis came out this far. That was what I remembered thinking, sitting there in my room with my nose pressed up against the glass, afraid to run after her, and not knowing what I'd say if she did. The white triangular sign on the top of the big yellow car glowed absurdly in the middle of the woods, not belonging.

I knew how it felt.

Now, I realized that my parents' escalating fights leading up to that day must have been *about* Foxwoods. About my father wanting to do something, to fight back, and my mother not wanting to turn her daughter into a warrior. She'd shown me precious little tenderness to my face, but it was strangely comforting, even now, to know that she cared for me in her own way.

"But you said…" I cleared my throat. "You said there's just us left. And the rest of the bloodline is gone. We can't…they're not going to listen to us."

"No," he said, his eyes hard and fixed, unblinking, on mine. "But they'll listen to you."

"They won't," I half-whispered, my voice refusing to cooperate now. "I don't know what kind of influence you think I have, but…"

My father's mouth quirked a little at the corner. "You don't know, do you? They're all berserkers. Every one of them. Steve, Andrea, Joe, your precious boss. All those guys at the shop. That's why they've taken such a liking to you. But that doesn't really matter. None of those people matter. We've got our ace in the hole."

My fists clenched reflexively in my lap.

"That Cole," my father said, still wearing his mask of a smile. "Did you think you could hide it from me? I can smell him on you."

Swallowing reflexively, I tried to stop my throat from closing up. "I…he…I don't…"

He put up a hand to stop me. "Don't. Please. I know how it is. It's only natural for someone like you. The instincts are strong, so you connect with these people like no one else can. Especially Cole. That creature's one of the strongest berserkers there is. But mentally, he's weak. He hates himself and he doesn't trust his clan. He senses that something's wrong. He knows how dangerous they are. All you have to do is let him believe that. Encourage him. Be his rock. Be the one person in the world that he can trust."

My father leaned forward in his seat. "He doesn't know what it means to be human. So teach him."

There wasn't enough air left in the room. My heartbeat pounded so hard that it felt like my whole body was shaking, as my head slowly tried to separate and float up to the ceiling.

"I can't," I said, hearing my own voice as a distant echo. "I don't know how."

"Yes you do," my father said. "You already are."

After I'd completely lost all ability to understand what my father was saying, he'd blabbered some nonsense about "giving me time to think," and walked out of my apartment. I sat there for a long while afterwards, not moving from where he'd left me.

It couldn't be real. It had to be some kind of cruel joke. But even my father didn't seem capable of this. Besides, it was too elaborate. He *must* really believe it.

After what I'd seen with my own eyes, how could I deny my father's story?

The facts, at least, seemed to explain many of the things I'd never been able to understand. About Douglas Mountain, about the people who lived here. No matter how many times he told me not to, I'd keep calling them "people." They simply were. He could choose not to see it, but I didn't have that luxury.

I was up all night, pacing and thinking, my mind running in circles. Before I knew it, the sun had risen high in the sky, and I still didn't have any answers.

When Cole called, I didn't pick up.

I had to gather my thoughts before I talked to him. There'd be no use pretending I was all right; I must look like I'd seen a ghost, and he'd be able to tell. Once he asked me what was wrong, I'd spill everything. I would have to beg off meeting with him today.

Naturally, being Cole, he didn't give me the chance.

He only called a few more times before I heard pounding at my door, and this time I was sure of who it was. I sat there, staring at the slightly vibrating wood, ignoring it for as long as I could force myself.

"Come on, Heather!" Cole's voice boomed. "I know you're in there."

I dragged myself over to the door, my feet as heavy as lead.

"Jesus," he said, when I finally yanked it open. "What happened, Heather?"

There wasn't any point in lying. Then again, there wasn't any point in telling the whole truth, either.

"Dad came over last night," I said. "Haven't seen him in - well, almost as long as I haven't seen you."

Cole reached for my arm, just resting his hand on it lightly. "Is everything okay?"

I nodded. "He just, you know…wanted to catch up, I guess."

Cole tilted his head at me. I was a terrible liar, but he wasn't going to push it.

Flopping down on the sofa, I let my eyes close for a few

moments. "It wasn't a coincidence, was it? Adanna coming here right after you left?"

He was silent for a while.

"No," he said, finally. I heard him sit down on the other end of the couch. "I was in the running to lead the clan. Everybody expected it. When I left, they had to scramble. Find somebody new. They're better off this way."

I had so many questions still, and so many that I didn't dare give voice to. I didn't know where to start, and I wasn't sure where I could stop, either.

Cole went on, after a deep sigh. "Now that I'm back, everybody seems to think I want to be the Alpha. They're not saying it, of course. Not in so many words. But it's obviously what they expected. I won't be able to convince them that I just missed…"

I held my breath for a moment.

"…everything," he finished, at last.

I opened my eyes.

"I'm assuming somebody has studied you guys," I said, staring at the ceiling. "Doctors, I mean. Scientists. Genetically speaking."

"Yeah," he said, after a pause. "Where's this coming from?"

"I've just been doing a lot of thinking," I said. "That's all. It's a lot to wrap my head around."

Cole cleared his throat. "I get it," he said. "Sorry. I just…I know it's a lot. I had some of the same questions when I first woke up in the middle of the woods, with a dead rabbit next to me."

The fear was almost palpable. He wasn't showing it on his face, or in his voice, but I felt it all the same.

I'm afraid. I don't know what happens when I'm like that, and I'm terrified I'll hurt somebody.

My subsconscious seemed to have developed a penchant for talking to me in Cole's voice. At least, I had to believe that's what that was.

"Woke up?" I echoed, looking at him. "You mean you don't remember what happens when you're…"

"No," he said. "Not really. Bits and pieces, sometimes. But it's foggy." He looked at me for a moment. "You want me to get out of here for a while? You look like you could use some rest."

I shook my head. There was no way I'd be able to switch off my brain and sleep, no matter how badly I wanted to.

"Can't sleep," I said, finally.

"I'm sorry." He scooted closer, resting his hand on my shoulder. "I know it's been a lot to handle, these past couple days. I wish I knew how to make it easier." He smiled a little. "I could go punch your dad in the face, if that would help."

I laughed. "Please don't. But thank you."

He may have been half-joking, but Cole knew almost every ugly detail of my childhood, and the way my father treated me. Every hurled insult, every broken door frame, every late night he never came home, and never called. Every jagged, fist-sized hole in the wall. Every time he made me feel like less than nothing.

It still made Cole angry, even now. I could feel it.

All I wanted to do was curl up against him and fall asleep, and not wake up for days. But what if my father was somehow right? What if sleeping next to a man who turned into a giant wolf with no consciousness and no memory actually *was* a bad idea?

This was insane. Every part of it was insane. In my current state, I could almost pretend it was all just a dream. Any minute now, I'd wake up.

Alone.

My defenses were low. Too low to fight the urge anymore. I wrapped my arms around Cole, pulling him close with a sudden movement.

"Ooof," he muttered, returning my embrace. "You sure you're okay, Sunshine?"

I nodded against his chest.

Being this close to him was overwhelming - but in a good way. His warmth, his scent, the feel of his body pushed everything else aside. I stopped worrying about what my father had said, and even my exhaustion started to ebb away slightly.

"Maybe I can help you relax," he murmured, against the side of my head.

I chuckled softly. "Smooth, Jackman. Really smooth."

I felt him smile. "But you didn't say no."

"Course not," I said. "I make it a personal policy to never turn down sexual favors."

He kissed me, slow and sweet, taking his time. I melted into it, letting him lie me down on the sofa and kiss his way down my body, undoing buttons and pushing aside fabric as he went. When he reached my jean shorts, I lifted my hips for him, and he slid them down, leaving my panties behind.

"Think you forgot something," I muttered.

"Did I?" He was probably grinning. I felt a light puff of air on the damp spot at the center of my panties - and shivered all over. A moment later, his lips followed, kissing and nuzzling me through the fabric. A warm tingling travelled straight from my core up to my heart, and I sighed.

His tongue followed, making little circles around my clit. Gasping, I rolled my hips. The fabric of my panties, wet and getting wetter, was spreading out the intensity of the sensations. I'd never felt anything quite like it.

Delicious tension built and built, and I found myself marveling at how different he could be, how different *we* could be. From our frantic coupling in the woods, to this - it was night and day, and I loved them both, almost as much as I loved…

Cole yanked my panties aside, and my train of thought derailed at the feeling of his tongue directly on my aching flesh. I groaned, bucking up to his mouth, my heart seizing with the overwhelming pleasure of my climax.

As my pulse slowed, my eyelids grew unbearably heavy. I felt myself grow weightless, and I realized Cole was lifting me, carrying me to my bed. When I tried to mutter something, he just kissed me on the forehead and curled up next to me under the covers.

That was the last thing I remembered, for a while.

Chapter Six

It was still light out when I woke up. Blinking sleepily, I instinctively cuddled up against Cole before I could remember everything that had happened.

Worry and confusion seeped back into my mind. Now that my head was slightly clearer, I realized that I needed to get as much information from Cole as I could. I had to understand what was going on, from his point of view - how much he knew about the clan and its history, and the warriors, too. But he was right - I was a terrible liar.

I'd have to tell him *some* of what my father told me. But none of that warrior bloodline nonsense about me. If he took it seriously, I had no idea how he'd react.

I laid there for what felt like ages, trying to work it out in my head. There was no way to say it that wouldn't at least pique his curiosity.

Honesty was the best policy. Up to a point.

When he finally woke up, blinking slowly, a smile started creeping across his face almost before he was completely conscious. I smiled back, kissing him on the tip of his nose.

He chuckled.

"Good morning," he murmured, slinging his arm in my general direction. I tucked it under my head, turning to look at him.

Immediately, his expression grew serious. "What's wrong?"

"My father knows about you," I said, simply.

Cole turned his head to look at me fully, frowning slightly. "Me?" he asked. "Or all of us?"

"All of you, I guess," I said. "I don't know. Not everything he said made a lot of sense."

He considered this for a second. "Well, not everything about us makes a lot of sense. I didn't think anybody else really knew about us, though."

Adanna would've told me. Wouldn't she? She trusts me.

Doesn't she?

These thoughts crept into my mind as if they were my own, but with Cole's voice. There was no mistaking it now. It was becoming more distinct, the more time I spent with him.

It couldn't be what I thought it was. It was impossible.

Almost as impossible as the idea of shapeshifters…

"He told me you…" I swallowed, hard. "…he said there used to be wars. A long time ago. Between the humans and the…" I hesitated, watching his face. "He called you 'berserkers.'"

Cole's forehead creased. He didn't say anything, just frowning slightly.

"I'm sorry," I said, quickly. "That's not like…a slur, is it?"

"Not…exactly," he responded, at last. "But it's very, you know…it's very strange. It's not a term people use nowadays."

"Right," I said. "I'd never heard it. Not that I…you know, not that I knew any of this was real. But I've heard of shapeshifters, werewolves, skin-walkers…"

"It's some kind of ancient word," he cut in. "Like maybe Greek, or something like that. I remember learning about it a long time ago. Some of the earliest shifters were fearsome warriors, before anybody understood much about it." He laughed slightly. "Not that we understand much about it now.

73

But, you know what I mean."

I picked up my phone and tapped the word into Google, feeling a tiny bit surreal about the whole thing. "Old Norse," I said, when I found it. "Supposedly Odin controlled them."

"That's right." Cole chuckled. "How could I forget. Good old Odin One-Eye."

Swallowing hard, I continued. "He said there was a lot of fighting. Between certain human warriors and the berserkers, and then…"

I took a deep breath.

"…they started, I don't know, selective breeding. Certain warriors were better at understanding the berserkers. So they picked those, and trained them from a young age, and made them have children. But it backfired."

Cole nodded. "I've heard the story," he said. "Rolf and Cecily. He was one of us, and she was a warrior for the commonfolk. They fell in love. They were just kids, but…" He stopped, frowning. "I still don't understand how your dad knows all these things. We keep them to ourselves."

I shrugged, feeling lightheaded again. "He didn't say. I don't know why he thought it was so important, suddenly."

Half-sitting up in bed, Cole blurted: "He's not one of us, is he? Another runaway? Like me?"

He actually looked excited by the prospect. My heart twisted. I wanted to tell him *no, no, he's dangerous, stay the fuck away from him*. But as long as he suspected my father might be a berserker, maybe he wouldn't suspect the opposite. It was safer this way.

"I don't know," I said. "I've never…I've never *changed*."

"It doesn't always pass down," he said. "Not when there's cross-breeding between us and the commonfolk. Sometimes the children change, sometimes they don't. But they're always special. The way you are with animals - maybe it's because you have just enough of our blood to make them understand you as their kin, but not enough to frighten them."

"It could be," I said, hoping against hope that this explanation might have some merit. But I knew my father wasn't one of them. If he was, I'd feel it. I wouldn't be so cold, and feel so alone, whenever I was with him.

"You've got to ask him," Cole insisted. "Or I will. It's important."

"Why?" I picked at the blanket, trying to appear ambivalent.

"Because, if you share our blood you can claim membership to the clan. Everybody would be so happy."

There was pleading, desperation in his eyes, and I started to understand. If I was one of them, maybe I'd be the new darling. Maybe they'd start paying a little less attention to him.

"I don't know," I said. "There has to be a reason he didn't tell me, if that's true."

"I'm sorry," said Cole, flopping back on his pillow, defeated. "I just thought it might be cool if you were. I know this is all new to you. You're going to want to take your time figuring it out."

"Yeah," I said. "Thanks." I let silence reign for a minute. "So what happened to Rolf and Cecily?"

"You mean, in the story?" Cole rolled his head from side to side, popping his neck softly. "These are all just really old, passed-down fairy tales, you know. I don't think any of it's real."

"Yeah," I said. "In the story."

"Well, they tried to run away together, but the warriors caught them. They said they'd kill Cecily if Rolf didn't agree to start fighting on their side. They kept her captive and had armed guards at the ready, constantly, just waiting for the order. So he did - and he was one of their best, so he devastated his own forces. Once the clan leaders saw what the warriors were willing to do, threatening one of their own - well, I guess you could say morale took a nosedive. They started to fear there was nothing they could do. They were losing. They were desperate. But the warriors refused to let them surrender, no matter what the concessions were. They just wanted a bloodbath.

"Finally, when they'd pushed us back to the very edges of our territories, they made an offer. If we agreed to stay on certain land, and never broach their borders, they'd let us live. They'd free Cecily and Rolf to go live their lives as they chose. The clan leaders accepted. They had no choice. Even the women and children were dying. So they signed the treaty in blood.

"Once it was done, the leader of the warriors turned to Cecily, lifted his axe, and beheaded her in a single stroke. 'This is what happens to all human traitors.' Rolf howled and raged, but he was chained. Back then, the warriors knew how to make chains that would hold even the strongest of us. They killed him too, in front of his father, who was one of the clan leaders.

"'We've done you a favor,' was all the leader of the warriors said. 'Remember this when you think of stepping your toe across these borders.'"

Cole half-smiled. "It's pretty brutal, but it makes a good point, I guess. No worse than one of the Grimm fairy tales."

"But there *are* territories," I said. "There was a treaty. In real life, I mean - wasn't there?"

He nodded. "Apparently. I'm sure the war was real, and that's how we ended up being stuck on these little scraps of land, but rest of it just sounds too ridiculous for me. Over the years, though, the warriors all disappeared. Eventually, once we realized the threat was disappearing, we started to take a little of our own back. There are some clans out there more superstitious than others, but mostly we've started expanding as much as we need to. And so far, no vicious magical warriors have come out of the woodwork to stop us."

He grinned, that same dazzling smile that usually made my heart melt, and made me weak in the knees. But now, I felt unsteady for an entirely different reason.

"What if they came back?" I asked, softly, before I could stop myself.

"Oh, Heather." Cole smiled, curling toward me and kissing me on the forehead. "Don't worry about that. They're long gone. There's nobody left who knows or cares about us anymore."

"Anybody know how to crank up the A/C in this place?" Cole addressed the question to the general populace. Most of them didn't look up. A few shrugged, glancing at each other.

We were in the Foxwoods clubhouse, waiting for the clan meeting to start. It wasn't quite what I'd expected, when I'd pictured it in my head. In fact, it looked exactly like any other community meeting - if I hadn't already known that all of these people occasionally turned into animals, I would never have guessed.

I fanned myself with a copy of the agenda, looking up at the front door when I heard it swing open.

Adanna walked into the room, with all her usual grace. Her vibrant burnt-orange skirt suit glowed against the deep brown of her skin. Arthur, on the other hand, looked like death. His suit, hair, and skin were all vaguely the same shade of pallid gray. He sat with lips pursed and fingers interlaced, refusing to get up and acknowledge Adanna until she cleared her throat.

"Oh," he said, finally, looking up. "Ms. Ogbuagu. How lovely to see you again."

"Charmed." Adanna's smile was frozen as she shook his hand and sat down next to him at the table.

"Nice weather we're having," said Arthur.

"Yes, lovely, isn't it?" Adanna smiled tolerantly. "I do love the weather as a topic. Don't you? It breaks the ice so well. Where I grew up, we had the same weather every day. Nothing to do but have actual conversations."

Arthur loosened his collar with a single finger. "Sounds nightmarish," he said. "I never could stand the heat."

Adanna's smile grew a little. "Yes," she said. "That doesn't surprise me in the least."

Chilly silence reigned at the head table, while a few more attendees filtered in. My eyes were jumping all over the room, trying to comprehend that every single one of these people guarded the same secret that Cole did. This whole room was full of bears, badgers and voles, maybe even some birds - deer? Bats? The possibilities were endless.

Beside me, Cole was all restrained energy. He hunched forward in his chair, elbows resting on his thighs, apparently trying to bore a hole in the wall with his eyes. Back in high school, this kind of thing would've bored him to tears. We'd pass sarcastic notes back and forth in assembly, and he'd quietly roll his eyes at anything that required him to sit still for very long. But today, he was almost vibrating. There was an undercurrent of frenetic energy in the room, and even Cole wasn't immune.

Because on some level, we all knew. This wasn't just about the fountain. It wasn't just about Foxwoods and Alki and me and Cole and everyone else who'd made our home in the foothills of Douglas Mountain. Something greater was at stake, and everyone in the room could feel it.

Finally, just as the big hand on the clock ticked another hour, Arthur Craven stood up and began to speak.

"I've called this meeting to order because so many of you -" here, he glanced over at the Alki Valley side of the room "- seemed to feel this was an issue worthy of the clan's attention. As you all know, there has been a great deal of discussion about the possibility of selling the land between Foxwoods and Alki Valley."

Adanna cleared her throat. "If I may, Mr. Craven, it's worth noting that you have already spoken to the commissioner about this issue, in your position as the community board leader of Foxwoods. But you did so without speaking to any of us first. Whether or not something is a 'clan issue' isn't a decision you are authorized to make on your own."

Arthur blinked, not looking at her. "I will admit, friends - there are times when the crossover between my public role as the Foxwoods community board president and the clan's community liaison often overlap. But that's neither here for there. Even if I had been acting as a spokesman for the clan, whose authorization do I need? Does anyone know the by-laws on this?"

He was addressing the crowd, apparently, but no one wanted to answer, their eyes downcast and shifting all over the room. "Anyone?" He smiled. "It seems Ms. Ogbuagu has neglected to bring a copy of the bylaws, but thankfully I have one with me. And if I can refer to the relevant passage - well, it seems that the community liaison has the right to make certain judgment calls when working under limited time constraints. And I've made no secret of my feelings on this issue."

Glancing around the room again, he continued.

"The fountain doesn't belong to us. The *land* doesn't belong to us. I know we've had our differences, but even my friends in Alki Valley will surely agree that the time's come to let go of childish superstitions. It's time to adapt or die. Our species has survived so many things; I think it would be tragic if a petty land dispute marked the beginning of the end."

Adanna's mouth was drawn into a thin line. "Don't you think that's a bit melodramatic, Arthur? We can adapt, but we also have to preserve what's important to us. Not all of us still believe in the old gods, but we've all stood near the fountain and felt its energy."

Here, Arthur let out a barely-restrained snort.

"We all know what it means to us," Adanna went on, ignoring

him. "And that's what is important. Not politics or petty arguments. If this is something we're willing to fight for, we have that right. And more than that, we have the right to make that decision as a clan. No one has the right to make it for us. Not me, not Arthur, and not the Commissioner."

Beside me, Cole was taut like a drawn bow. He looked like he wanted very much to speak, but something was holding him back. I felt his energy coursing through my own veins, leaving me tingling and a little bit breathless. I was momentarily taken with the insane urge to try and drag him into the supply closet for a quickie, but I was thankfully able to restrain myself.

In the crowd, a young woman tentatively raised her hand.

"Yes?" said Arthur. "Ms. Woodrow?"

"I'm just wondering," she said, her voice soft, but firm all the same. "I'm just wondering if you took any proposals to the Commissioner that would allow us to take control of the land. We've put all this sweat and hard work into maintaining the trails and the fountain, maybe they would let us buy it at a discount. If everyone pitched in -"

Arthur made a slight noise, and the young woman stopped talking. She bit her lip, her brown eyes casting downwards, long waves of chestnut hair falling down to partially hide her face.

"As much as I would love to hold a bake sale," said Arthur, "and reclaim to land for our own, we have to think about this practically. The whole county is running out of funds. That affects us, too - as much as like to occasionally pretend that we exist in a vacuum. The sale of the land will generate important revenue. To buy it at a discount doesn't benefit anyone, even if the county agreed to the sale. And why would they? Quite frankly, we can't compete with the land developers who are vying for this property."

"Excuse me," said a man, sitting next to the chestnut-haired woman. He was lanky and handsome, but a little shorter than

Cole, dirty-blonde with eyes that shone fiercely as he spoke. "But I think we'd all appreciate it if you could refrain from patronizing us when we try to participate."

Arthur's face twitched. "I sincerely apologize if I've caused your lady friend any offense," he said. "But I suspect that very few of you have an understanding of how local politics work. We can't buy the land. It's not that simple."

"Forgive me, Arthur," said Adanna, standing up. "But we're to just take your word on this? Without speaking to the commissioner ourselves?"

"Well, yes," he said, turning quickly, and actually *looking* at her for the first time since the meeting starting. "Unless you care to explain to the commissioner exactly who you are, and why you -"

"I'm a concerned citizen," Adanna cut in. "A respected member of the Alki Valley community. They don't need to know anything more than that. Don't invent excuses."

He threw his hands up in the air. "Fine!" he snapped, sitting back down. "Go and talk to her, then. You're more than welcome. But what exactly is your plan? They're already well aware that this land means something to the people. But you can't pay teacher's salaries and re-pave roads on memories of forest magicks."

"Listen," came Cole's voice, startling me enough to jump a little in my chair. He straightened slightly, but he was still leaning forward. "I think we all know how you feel about the spirit world, Arthur. I'm no great believer in things I can't see, but that's not what we're debating here."

"Ah," said Arthur, smiling wanly as he turned to face our side of the room. "Cole, isn't it?"

Cole just sat stock-still, meeting his cold gaze. "You know my name."

"So nice to have you back," Arthur said. "Well, you've been away for a while, I dare say - since you were practically just a boy.

I'd respectfully disagree with you. People's feelings towards this forest, and this fountain, have everything to do with their spiritual beliefs. We can't discuss one without discussing the other."

"Well, do you think we can discuss one without *mocking* the other?" Cole countered, his voice loud, but steady. "We're not going to get anywhere if you keep talking like that."

Arthur blinked a few times, rapidly. "I'm sorry," he said, still smiling blankly. "Are you really criticizing *my* tone?"

"Let him speak," said Adanna, quietly. "He has as much right as you."

Arthur was shaking his head, before she even finished. "No, no, Adanna, you see, that's where you're wrong. Cole forfeit that right when left. He could have been in your seat now, but he gave that up. He hasn't lived here in ten years."

"Yes, but he grew up here," Adanna said. "Just as you did. A qualification that even *I* - as you're so fond of pointing out - do not have."

What the *hell* were they talking about? Was Cole really supposed to be the clan's leader before be left? My head was swimming, and I stole a glance in Cole's direction, but he was staunchly refusing to look at me.

"What about Heather?" Arthur gestured broadly towards me, and I felt my throat start to close up. "She has the unique advantage of being both an Alki native, born and raised, *and* someone from outside of the clan. And she's been here all along. I'd be very interested to hear her perspective on this land sale."

"Don't bring her into this," Cole growled, half-standing.

"Cole," I said, firmly. "It's fine." Clearing my throat, I stood up, slowly, mindful of all the eyes that were suddenly fixed on me. "I would hate to see that forest go away," I said. "Of course. And the fountain particularly. It's always been very special to me. But I understand the practical concerns too. I don't have any answers. I wish I did. But I think the fountain is special, no matter who you are, or what you believe in."

I sat down, heart pounding. Arthur's irritation was palpable, but Adanna was smiling slightly.

"Thank you for sharing, Heather," she said. "I think I speak for everyone when I saw that your input is very valuable here. You're as much a part of this community as we are."

Arthur cleared his throat slightly. "Indeed," he said. "All the same, as Heather has so concisely stated, she doesn't have any answers. None of us do."

"We don't need answers," Cole said, and once again, all heads turned towards us. "We just need to fight back. Create a gridlock. We can't stop them, but we can slow them down so much that it amounts to the same thing." He smiled, slowly. "How's that for politics, Arthur?"

At the head table, Arthur went white as a corpse, then rapidly flushed red. "These things all take time," he spluttered. "Time and money and energy that we don't have. Who's going to -"

"I will," said Cole, simply. "You won't even have to lift a finger. Even you can't object to that."

"I *can*," said Arthur, "because it's a waste of your time, too. If you want to help the clan, you might want to consider starting with the broken leadership structure you left in your wake, because you refused to accept your birthright."

His voice had grown darker and colder as he spoke, something beyond the usual light contempt in his tone. I felt my blood chill in my veins.

Adanna spoke again, finally. "What's done is done," she said. "He's back now, and he's offering to help solve this problem, Arthur. I don't see any reason to argue about the past. The future is what's important."

"*Exactly*," said Arthur. "But how are we supposed to move into the future if we can't let go of our past? The world is changing.

We have to keep up with it."

"The world is always changing," Cole insisted, leaning forward in his chair. "The world always changes around us. But we don't change. Not where it counts."

"A very pretty ideal," said Arthur. "Where did you hear that from - your grammar school teacher?"

"Enough!" Adanna's voice rang out in the hall. All heads turned, and the only noise was someone's partially-stifled cough. "I've only heard one person suggest a solution so far, and I think we should put it to a vote. All in favor of Cole heading this project, please raise your hands."

About half of the people in the room lifted their hands. Adanna and Arthur both counted silently, their eyes darting around the room.

"All against?" Arthur asked, eyes narrowing.

"So that's settled," said Adanna, a moment later. "Cole will develop our strategy to fight the sale of the land. He'll bring a proposal next month. Meeting adjourned."

Most of the attendees filtered out shortly after that, but Cole was quickly cornered by a few people I didn't really recognize. I kept my distance, noting the low, confidential tones of their voices. Whatever it was, I wasn't invited to that conversation.

Adanna came over to me, with an armful of papers. "Thank you for coming," she said. "I hope you're not horribly traumatized."

I laughed. "Looks like we all survived. For now."

"Indeed." She glanced over at Cole. "Arthur might have an aneurysm, but that's a problem for another day."

Clearing my throat, I shifted my purse from one shoulder to the other. "I'm honestly surprised that Cole stepped up," I said. "I mean, I'm glad. But I'm surprised."

She nodded. "He's still ambivalent about getting too involved with the clan. That boy is confused. He has been for a long time. But I think the longer he stays here, with us - and with you - the more everything will start to make sense. He just needs to accept the reality of who he is, and *what* he is."

"He almost seems…" I considered my words carefully before I spoke. "…frightened by it. You know?"

She nodded. "He never learned to control it. Not the way most of us do. It's very difficult when you're a teenager, but as you grow older, you learn. It's like anything else." She smiled. "Very poor self-control when you're young. We are no different from the commonfolk in that regard. But Cole left before he had a chance. The changing is still a very frightening thing for him."

"He doesn't seem to remember anything that happens when he's…changed." I was choosing my words carefully, even though Adanna had never struck me as someone to get offended by my staggering ignorance of shifter culture.

"It's like that, at first," she said, nodding. "It takes practice to remember. It's a little bit like ludic dreaming."

"So is he really not in control of himself?" I nibbled on my lower lip, unsure if I really wanted an answer. "I mean, he doesn't seem to think he is."

Adanna's mouth twisted slightly. "Yes and no," she said, finally. "It's…hard to say. He won't talk much about it. If he'd tell me more, I could try to help him, but…you know how he is."

I didn't particularly like the sound of that.

"It's simply a matter of connecting the two state of consciousness," she went on. "He thinks he's not conscious as himself when he's changed, but he is. The memory is the problem. It only works one way. As a wolf, he has all his human memories, in some form or another. But as a man, he has to learn how to access them."

"Oh," I said, not really understanding, but not wanting to ask any more questions.

I refused to accept that my father was right about him. Cole was *more* than human, not less. I'd seen him change in front of me, and all he did was protect me. I had nothing to be afraid of.

I had to believe that.

Chapter Seven

There was one undeniable fact that I had to confront.

The closer I got to Cole, the more I was separating him from his clan. From the only people who really understood him, and could help him. My father had made that abundantly clear. Whenever I was wrapped up in Cole's arms, I could practically hear him cheering from the sidelines. It made me sick.

But just like always, I couldn't stay away.

After the meeting, Cole hadn't come home with me. I'd half-expected it, but I'd come out of the bathroom after my conversation with Adanna to find him gone. He didn't call that night, or the next morning.

And so it begins.

I told myself he was busy strategizing, or gathering signatures, or just whatever the hell it was he planned to do about the land sale. I'd been a little concerned that he'd start hassling me to ask my father more questions about my origins, but I would have preferred that to his complete radio silence.

I kept on going to work, going through the motions, and trying not to notice how much time was passing. Obviously, Steve and Joe knew he was in town by now. But they didn't bring it up, and I didn't, either. The last thing I wanted to do was start asking around - "hey, have you seen my ex-boyfriend? I was kind of hoping to spend the night with him again…"

Finally, on the third night, when I was starting to suspect it was all just a dream, I felt a strong pull towards the fountain on my walk home. Stronger than usual.

And then I smelled it.

I smelled *him*.

As I walked, I tried to classify that scent. It was just Cole. Not sandalwood or pine or the smell of the earth just before a rainstorm. It was unmistakably masculine, mouth-watering, and unlike anything I'd ever experienced in my life.

He was standing in the clearing when I reached it, in front of the fountain, close enough to reach out and dip his hands into the water. But he wasn't.

"Get my message?" he asked, quietly.

"Oh." I walked a little closer. "Is that what that was?"

"Mmhmm." He wasn't looking at me. "You could've mentioned that you can read my thoughts."

What the fuck kind of person keeps that a secret? he demanded, inside my head.

I cringed. "I didn't think that's what it was!" I insisted. "It seemed nuts. I just ignored it. I thought it was my own subconscious talking to me, or…something."

"Right." He let out a bark of laughter. "Well, Adanna's up my ass now, wanting to know why I'm not asking her for help, if I'm so afraid I'm gonna hurt somebody. You don't have to air my dirty laundry all over the clan. Besides, I never said that. I never even *thought* it."

"But you are," I hazarded. "Aren't you?"

"Wouldn't you be?" he almost shouted, sending the few birds in the clearing scattering.

"I don't know, Cole!" I crossed my arms, turning to face him. "I don't know anything! I learned about all this shit last week, and I have no idea how to process it all, and I'm sorry if I betrayed your confidence, but I was scared too. I don't know what to expect. I don't know who you really are. All those times you claimed you didn't keep any secrets from me, you were lying. Even ten years ago, I didn't really know you. And now? I know you even less." I exhaled, long and bitter.

Cole was bending forward now, resting his hands on the edge of the fountain, his head hanging loose.

"I'm sorry, Heather," he said. "This is fucked up. I know it's fucked up. But, I mean - what are we doing here?"

"You mean us, specifically?"

"I mean us, specifically." He glanced over at me, finally. "Are you shivering?"

"No," I insisted. "But it is getting a little chilly. Can we go somewhere else and talk?"

He swallowed audibly. "Back to your place? We don't seem to get much talking done there."

"So what?"

Shrugging, he took a step back. "I don't know if it's a good idea."

I don't want to hurt you again.

"Come on," I said. "Let's just go. I promise this isn't a nefarious plan to seduce you."

Cole was silent on the whole walk home, and he didn't start talking again until he was flopped out on my sofa. I sat there patiently for a moment, until he began.

"I don't even know what the fuck I'm doing here," he said, staring at the ceiling. "I came back because I didn't know what else to do. But now I'm mired in all this political bullshit, everything I wanted to get away from. Fuckhead Arthur talking about my birthright. Like we're in fucking *Game of Thrones*. I didn't want to be the Alpha, why should I have to be? Just because my father was? They're doing just fine without me. Clearly."

He let out a bitter laugh.

"I was everybody's favorite. The star kid with a bright future. I know, I know, boo hoo, how could I stand it?" His mouth twisted into a joyless smile. "But the *pressure*. Everybody was sure I'd be the next Alpha. By the time I was ten years old, I started to feel like the whole rest of my life was going to be planned out for me. I wasn't going to have a choice.

"Oh, sure, people asked me what I wanted - and of course I went along with it. I basked in the attention. I wanted to make everyone happy. But the older I got, the more trapped I started to feel. This town. This life. These people. All of it - I wanted to leave it behind, even if meant living in secret, and never being able to truly share my life with someone. I mean, when do you bring up the fact that you're a werewolf? Third date? Two-month anniversary? Right before you move in together?"

I looked down at my hands. "I mean, before the wedding night, ideally."

He snorted. "But that's the thing. There was no option for me to live my life with the others. You don't just leave, and abandon your clan - the other clans wouldn't have me. That's how rivalries start. And we can't afford any more of those. It's bad enough as it is, with Foxwoods and Alki. And we're supposed to be in the same clan. It's even worse when there are fewer ties. Maybe I could find a clan who wants to piss off mine, so they'll take me in - but that's a political act in and of itself. I was sick of all that. I didn't want any part of it. I just wanted to live somewhere. Free from all of this bullshit."

"We all put up with a certain amount of bullshit," I pointed out.

Cole looked at me, his expression unreadable. "Some more than most," he said. "I never wanted to leave you behind, but I had to."

My eyes started to feel a little misty. I cleared my throat "I would've followed you," I said, quietly, still looking down at my hands. "Anywhere."

"I know, Sunshine." His voice was soft, and a little wistful. "That's the problem."

"I don't really see how that's a problem," I said, looking back down. When I met his eyes, the urge was too strong. The urge to just end this conversation now, silence it with a kiss, to lose myself in him for a few more hours and stop worrying about anything. But we couldn't keep ignoring this.

Whatever it was.

"I would have ruined your life too," he said. "Along with mine. It wasn't fair. We were…" He let out a long breath. "I know the good times were good, but don't you remember how bad it got? We fought dirty. Both of us. It wasn't your fault and it wasn't mine. We didn't know better. Didn't know much of anything, except how to hurt each other."

"We would've figured it out." Tears were welling in my eyes now, and I tried hard to fight the thickness in my voice. "We could have grown up together."

"And resented each other," he said. "Believe me, Heather, that was all I wanted. To tell you my secret, and take you with me. But think of what that would have been like. Really. Both of us, just clinging to each other because we felt like we had no choice. That's no way to live."

Thing was, I never knew anymore. Which version of the past was real? Sometimes I remembered it like he said, fighting all the time and lashing out just to feel something. Even our happiness was sad and desperate and hard-won. Other times, I remembered it like a little slice of heaven. So perfect and sweet that it hurt my heart to think about.

The reality of it must be somewhere in between. But I couldn't be sure. If even my own memories couldn't agree with each other, what hope did I have of figuring anything out? *Ever?*

Grief and confusion were swelling inside of me, and the tears finally started to spill down my cheeks. I didn't sniffle, didn't make a single sound to betray that I was crying, but Cole still twisted around and took my face in his hands.

"Hey, hey," he said. "Stop it. Don't. Please don't be upset. I just...I just wanted you to understand why I left. I didn't mean to...shit." His eyes pleaded with mine. "Please, I swear I didn't mean to hurt you."

"I don't know why you had to break up with me," I whispered, between hiccups. "We could've at least had those few months together."

His face hardened a little. "It was too much," he said. "I started doubting. Every time I was around you, I got close to just spilling it. Telling you everything. That's one of the cardinal rules, Heather - you never, *ever* tell the commonfolk about what we can do. Some even believe it's believe it's wrong to change in front of them, even if it's life-or-death. In some clans, I would've been excommunicated for what I did to save you."

"What you did to *save* me?" I jerked back, pulling my face away from his hands. "He only got like that because of you. I've walked through there a thousand times with cougars following me. He didn't want to hurt me. It was *you*."

He jumped to his feet, startling me half to death, and started prowling around the room. "That's the problem, isn't it?" He laughed harshly, raking his hands through his hair. "You think you want to be with me, even if it means I'll make your life worse. You'll swear up and down you don't care. It doesn't matter. Then it happens, you actually see how I'm putting you in danger, and it just makes you mad." He stopped and looked at me, his blue eyes now cloudy with frustration and sadness. "You're mad at me because you know I'm right."

"You're not right about everything," I insisted. "Okay, so maybe we don't go on hikes together around here. Maybe that's a sacrifice we have to make. But it's not like you're going to hurt me, just because you change. Adanna said that you're conscious, even if it seems like you're not."

He laughed bitterly. "Sure," he said. "That's what they tell you. But whenever it happens, whenever an innocent commonfolk gets hurt by one of us, the ruling's always the same. Mind you, it doesn't happen often - at least, not that we know about. But it *does* happen. It doesn't matter to the police - it just goes down in their records as 'mauled by a wild animal.' But inside the clans, it has to be dealt with. They have to stand trial. And every single one of them claims the same thing.

"'I didn't know what I was doing. I woke up covered in blood.' They're hoping to appeal to the jury's pity, because they know every single one of us has had it happen, only we got lucky. It turned out it was just an animal. But it never works, because the jury's too scared to admit the possibility. They have to believe it's not possible. We all do. Otherwise, everything people fear about us is true."

My father's words were echoing in my ears.

Not human.

No. I refused to believe it.

"What are you saying, then?" I demanded, sitting up straighter. "You came back here just to…fuck me a few times, and then what? We can't be together, because you're scared?"

"We can't be together because we shouldn't be together." Pain and regret was etched across his face when he looked at me. "Heather, honestly, if any sane, objective person looked at our history together - what do you think they'd say? That it's a *good idea* for us to try again?"

"I don't know," I admitted. "All I know is, I never stopped thinking about you. Not for one single day since you left."

"Of course you never stopped thinking about me," he said, bitterly. "Nobody ever gets sick of something they can't have."

My heart twisted in my chest. There was nothing I could say to him, nothing I could promise. He was too smart for that. He was too smart for a lot of things.

"You know, you're right," I said. "Maybe it's all fake. Maybe I don't even know *what* I feel. Everything could go to shit. So you might as well not even try, right? I mean, why put yourself through all that?"

He gave me a look, but I refused to let it shut me up.

"Maybe it's better not to do anything," I said, sitting up straighter, emboldened by my own words. "Maybe you're right. Just run away. Run away from me, run away from being the Alpha. It's better that way, isn't it? Save everybody from yourself. You're so *brave*, Cole. What a selfless guy you are."

Jumping to his feet, he leaned over me, snarling. "You don't know what the fuck you're talking about."

His heavy breathing was…distracting, to say the least. Adrenaline was zinging through my veins, and it was only a matter of time before urge started to take over my better judgment. I took a deep breath and tried to focus.

"Exactly," I said. "You know everything. You've got it all figured out."

He slammed his hand down on the arm of the sofa, and I felt the reverberations, but I didn't flinch. "It's so fucking easy to sit where you are, and tell me what you think I should do with my life. Come talk to me after the first time you've felt your body get ripped apart and re-made into something you don't recognize. Something terrible that only knows the smell of blood. Come talk to me the first time you wake up covered in it, and all you can do is pray it didn't come out of a human being. The first time you have to spend all day searching for a mutilated deer carcass in the woods, so you'll know exactly what kind of monster you are - come and tell me how easy it is. Come and tell me I'm a coward for running away. Say it to my face, Heather."

A dull, throbbing ache was starting to spread through my body. I suddenly remembered what he'd said to me:

Every time there's a full moon. Any time we feel we're in danger. And sometimes, just when we're really, really angry...

The fury on his face was slowly melting away, replaced by something worse.

Fear.

He reared up, backed away, not stopping until he was flat against the wall. His pupils dilated.

"Heather," he said, his voice suddenly hoarse. "Get out. Go. You have to leave."

He really thinks he might hurt me.

"No," I said, standing up and taking one step towards him. My whole body was shaking, but I didn't falter. Pure terror seized my heart, and I couldn't tell if it was his, or mine.

It's both. That's your curse.

"You have to." He swallowed hard, his eyes darting wildly around the room. "Please. I can't stop it."

"You can," I said, taking another step closer, though every cell in my body was screaming: *run away. Run away and don't look back.* "You can, and you will. Adanna told me. You just have to stop being afraid."

He groaned, his head pitching back, his fingers scrabbling at the wall. I felt the stab of pain, too, right in my chest. Like a dagger to the heart. But I only stumbled a little, and I kept walking.

"I know you won't hurt me," I said. "I know you won't let it happen. Even if you change."

Cole licked his lips, staring at me with eyes that were already starting to take on a different shape in some subtle, indescribable way. "I won't know who you are," he whispered.

By now, my face was just inches from his. I took one step closer until our bodies were pressed together, until I could feel every straining muscle as he fought to regain control.

"I won't let you forget," I whispered back, leaning in and capturing his mouth with a kiss.

This time he groaned for a different reason, his arms closing around me a squeezing tight. Almost too tight. Almost. I let my fingers run through his hair, and when my ribs started to ache, I grabbed on tightly by the roots and tugged. His grip loosened.

The transformation had halted for now, or at least slowed. I could feel it in my own body as much as he felt it in his. And even though I wasn't sure this would work, I had to believe that it would. Otherwise, he was right. How could I live with an uncontrollable monster? How could I love someone I had to keep in a cage once a month, and would destroy me if he broke free?

He kissed me back savagely, grabbing my wrists and flipping us around. Pressing his body hard against mine, he caged me against the wall, and I felt another shudder of his transformation going through him. Fear spiked in my chest, but there was no turning back now.

Finally, he pulled away, his chest heaving. There was something wild in his eyes, changing them in some way I couldn't quite describe. As he stood there, his shoulders seemed to broaden, his hands flexing and growing, tendons stretching the skin. He'd let go of my arms, but I still felt rooted to the spot.

He stared at me, and I stared back.

The light of recognition was still in his eyes. I had nothing to be afraid of. At least, not for now.

But something was holding him back, and it wasn't his willpower. I licked my lips, lust tingling in every part of my body, from my fingertips to my toes to the roots of my hair. I laid my hand on Cole's chest, feeling the burning heat radiating off of him.

Any other time, he'd be kissing me breathless, not even giving me a chance to think or hesitate. So what was different now?

He was different. The beast inside was taking control, and there was only one thing that it understood.

Instantly, me knees felt weak. I wished he would just *tell* me what he wanted, but I wasn't sure he could speak anymore. And he didn't have to say it - I knew.

Every hint of embarrassment melted away as I turned my back to him, walking up to the dining room table until my hips were up against the wood. I heard a soft growl from behind me, sending a shiver of anticipation through me. Leaning forward, I popped the button of my jeans, unzipping them slightly as I presented myself to him.

Cole came on like a hurricane.

With a snarl, he was on top of me, pressing me hard into the unforgiving wood. His fingers felt strange and inhuman as they curled around my waistband, yanking my jeans and panties down in one jerk. I hardly had a chance to take a single breath before he was inside me, his length feeling different too - thicker, longer, throbbing with wordless need.

But I was ready.

He slammed into me over and over, hard and deep, wrenching sobs of pleasure from deep inside my chest. My fingers scrabbled at the smooth wood of the tabletop as he bent me over even further, curling his body over mine, almost protectively. But he never let up his brutal pace.

I couldn't catch my breath, and I wasn't sure I wanted to. The frantic chaos of our mating thrilled me, and even the sharp jab of the wood against my hipbones felt like impossible bliss.

Cole's hands, covering mine on the table, changed a little more. As his fingers lengthened, nails slowly curling and thickening, he clutched down into the wood, and his newly-developed claws left gouges in the finish.

The only sounds he made were pants and growls, somehow even filthier than his usual dirty talk. Every time I breathed, it came out in a moan. Inside, I felt molten, and my inner muscles clenched down on Cole's cock with each movement.

I could feel his hot breaths on the back of my neck. He lowered his face down to nuzzle against it, the beginnings of his fur rasping against my skin, alongside his usual stubble. His teeth scraped against the sensitive spot behind my ear, and I shivered.

Then, they sank in.

They were just slightly sharper than normal, not quite enough to break the skin, but the delicious ache sent a shiver through me. My head spun. He was claiming me.

I remembered what he'd said in front of the mirror.

You're mine.

Inside, he swelled even more. A deep growl came from the back of his throat, rumbling through his chest and into mine, and with a few more thrusts, he stilled.

For a moment we were both suspended there, unmoving, silent except for our breathing.

He was still growing inside of me, bigger and thicker, and faster, and then I remembered something I had read about wolves, and I was suddenly afraid. But the pressure wasn't painful. It was something else entirely. It was an exquisite sensation of fullness, beyond what I'd ever wanted or imagined wanting.

I groaned, the sensations too intense to bear - but at the same time, I never wanted it to stop. None of it. The lingering sting from his bite, press of his hips against my ass, and the persistent swell of his cock deep inside. I was pulsing, aching, stretched to my limit. Something was building in waves, a pleasure unlike anything I'd experienced before.

And then I exploded.

Later I would remember screaming his name as I was overtaken with bliss, almost terrifying in its intensity, strong enough that I actually thought I might lose consciousness.

Just when I thought I couldn't bear it any longer, the sensations started to ebb. Cole was shaking, his claw-nails digging deeper into the abused wood as he spilled deep inside me. It felt like it went on endlessly, but the swelling inside seemed to have reached its peak. I relaxed slightly, just waiting for it to wane.

For a long time, we just breathed together.

By the time he pulled away, his hands had returned to their usual shape and size. I stood up, unsteadily, holding myself upright on the table, before giving up and plopping down on one of the chairs.

Cole wasn't looking at me.

"That was very stupid."

His tone was utterly flat and emotionless. All the pent-up emotions welled in my throat, but I refused to cry. I just sat there, silent, willing myself to be strong. Without looking up at him, all I could see was his lower half, and his hands that were balled into tight fists.

"I could've killed you," he said, and the self-loathing was so palpable that I couldn't hold back my tears anymore. But I turned my eyes to the table, staring at its glossy surface and trying hard not to remember how it had felt, pressing against my pelvis while he fucked me.

"But you didn't," I managed to whisper, without my voice breaking.

He let out a harsh laugh. "You think that makes it better? Like this is some kind of triumph? Like I'm an alcoholic and I managed to walk past a bar without going inside? Good job. I've managed not to kill someone today. Maybe the next time I feel like I'm about to change into an uncontrollable rage-beast, I should just call my sponsor."

"Adanna said she could help you!" I shouted, suddenly, jumping to my feet and staring him down. He didn't blink. "She said there's no reason for it to be this way. If you really think you could hurt someone, if you really think you're capable of killing me, then what the fuck is wrong with you? Why don't you let her teach you how to control it?"

The sobs were escaping my throat now, and I couldn't stop them. All I could do was try to talk around them.

"Killing me isn't what scares you," I said. "There's something else that scares you more. And I'm not sure I want to know what it is."

For a long time, all I heard was the sound of my own heartbeat.

Then, I heard the sound of his retreating footsteps, and the creak of the door as it swung open. The heavy *thunk* as it closed.

But I didn't look up, and my eyes swam in tears.

Chapter Eight

Had I really spent the better part of my night trying to convince Cole Jackman *not* to break it off with me?

I really was playing into my father's hands.

Cole had given me an out - and a damn good one, but I refused to take it. The absolute last thing I needed to do was stay close to him, and keep on stoking his doubts and fears with my very presence.

Sitting at the scarred dining table after a few hours of fitful sleep, I stared at my phone. If I just skipped town and never came back, would Cole ever bother to call and find out what happened to me? Or would he be glad that he could finally stay in his beloved Alki Valley without having to deal with me?

My phone buzzed. I didn't recognize the caller ID, but after I looked at the message, I remembered that my father had asked for my number before he left. And I didn't have the good sense to give him a fake one.

How are things going?

I deleted the message, and shoved my phone in my pocket.

There was only one way to get out of this situation. But I'd be damned if I was going to pull a Cole Jackman. I was going to talk to him first - as much as I just wanted to run away.

My phone buzzed again. This time, I knew the number.

We should talk. Meet at the fountain?

He was practically handing me the opportunity on a silver platter. I couldn't say no.

Yeah, be right there.

I walked slowly, like I was heading to my own funeral. Cole was already there when I approached the clearing.

"Heather," he said, his voice quiet and rough. "Yesterday…I don't know what happened. I'm sorry."

"No, *I* am." I couldn't look at him. "You were right. It was stupid. You were right about everything."

Cole took a step forward. "Heather - baby - no. I wasn't. I really wasn't." Desperation was starting to creep into his voice. "I've been bitter and I've been afraid. But that's not worth ruining something like…"

Finally, I dragged my eyes up to his face. "Something like *what*, Cole? Like what we used to have? Did you already forget how much we hurt each other? It was all you could talk about last night."

A part of me still believed it. That we were doomed from the start, cursed to always be drawn to each other, but never able to really love each other. Not the way we should. There would always be anger and resentment and sadness and fear.

He was the best mistake I ever made. But that didn't make him any less of a mistake.

"Sunshine, listen to me," he pleaded, reaching out to touch my shoulder. When I didn't react, he withdrew his hand, biting his lip before speaking again. "It was different. With you there, it's different. I can control it. I didn't feel like I was fading. The whole time, I was awake. I knew who I was. *And I knew who you were.*"

I shook my head, trying to turn away, but he didn't let me.

"Listen," he said. "Listen. I was wrong. I was confused, but I'm not anymore. All these years, I've been telling myself that I left so I wouldn't hurt you anymore. And I almost believed it. But the truth is, I just didn't want to face up to it. I'd *already* hurt you and I couldn't stand it, so I ran away. It's the most cowardly thing you can do - breaking up with someone, just to try and shrug off the responsibility of breaking their heart. Like it undoes the damage. I've realized that now, day by day, a little more every time I look at you."

He took a deep breath, his eyes fixed on mine. I tried to blink away the tears, but more just kept coming to replace them.

"It doesn't matter anymore," I finally whispered, pulling away.

Tell him. Say it. Say the words.

I don't love you anymore.

But I couldn't. The heartache and confusion on his face was already too much to bear.

"Heather, *please*," he implored, reaching out for me. I pretended not to see, eyes downcast. "Just - tell me what's really going on. I know there's something you're not telling me, and I don't know why, but…please. I've trusted you with every secret I have. You have to trust me."

"You don't understand." Tears streamed down my face, and I couldn't stop them. "I'm so sorry, Cole. I wanted…I wanted this to work out. But it's not. It's just…it's just not."

"NO!" His voice was louder, somehow wilder, than an ordinary person's. I thought he'd change, right in that moment - but he just stood there, anger and heartbreak warring on his face. "No, Heather. No. I won't let you do this. You spent all this time, trying to break down my defenses, trying to convince me that we could have something. And now you just want to walk away from it? You're going to leave me like this?"

I really was the scum of the earth. I'd left him raw and defenseless, just like my father wanted. But it had to end here. I couldn't keep doing this.

"Please," I begged, stumbling forward, feeling his own grief collide with mine, make my heart collapse. I lost my balance and fell down heavily on my knees. "Please, Cole, just go back to your people. Your clan needs you, and I can't be a part of that. They love you. They understand you. I'll never be able to get that close."

Something dawned on his face. "Is that was this is about? My clan? Heather, they can't replace you. It's different. But please don't…don't blame them, don't resent them, what's going on between us is something completely separate."

"It's not," I insisted, managing to talk through the sobs that were wracking my body. "I can't…please, Cole. I can't explain any more. Just trust me. I have to leave. You have to forget about me."

"You can't," he said. "I won't let you."

I stared up at him, my hands buried in the dirt, anger roiling with my grief. "You can't stop me."

In another moment he was down on his knees in front of me, grabbing the sides of my face, raising me up for a brutal, punishing kiss. Cold fat raindrops fell on my scalp, and I curled my arms around his neck, clutching, clawing, smearing dirt across his back.

He finally pulled away, gasping, and I could have sworn his eyes were a little red.

"I know I broke your heart," he said, his voice fading into the heavy splatter of the rain. "But you can't keep punishing me forever."

"I'm not punishing you," I insisted, barely stifling a sob. "I'm trying to save you."

He shook his head, desperately. "I don't need to be saved, Heather. I just need you."

Fuck everything.

Fuck this war, fuck the warriors, fuck my father for ruining my one chance at happiness. Fuck me for taking this war, and making it all about my stupid

feelings. Fuck Cole for refusing to let go.
  Fuck the rain.

He overtook me, and I let myself be overtaken. Another kiss, this one desperate, hungry, bending me backwards and pushing me down into the earth. I didn't fight it. I didn't even try.

I tasted the saltiness of tears, and I didn't know whose they were. With a growl, he reared back and yanked my jeans down, popping one of the buttons so that it bounced and skittered away on the pine needles. The heat was rising and I felt it boiling through my blood, burning on my skin. It was actually surprised when each falling raindrop didn't sizzle and turn to steam just from touching my flesh. Cole turned me into a living breathing fever, with no thought, just burning desire.

He lowered his head down to my sex and licked, long and hard, his tongue stiff and angry and so unlike his usual gentle caresses. It worked. My body stiffened in pleasure almost immediately, a quick jolt of unexpected climax rocketing through every nerve ending. A moment later he slammed into me, *god, how can he possibly be so hard already, oh god -*

I felt him grow longer, thicker, inside of me. Instantly I thought of our last encounter, over the dining table, which still bore gouges from his claws. But this was different. The transformation was only just beginning, driven forward by our frantic coupling.

Above me, his face was contorted into a snarl. I watched as his eyes changed, not in shape or color, but changed all the same.

This is it. This is how it's meant to be.

I could never shake that feeling when we were together, especially when we were together like this, and I tried to tell myself it was just hormones and desire running wild. I could ignore it. I *should* ignore it. Even as I thrashed and moaned underneath him, even as he licked up the side of my neck with a tongue that grew rougher every moment, even as he clawed the earth and his groans became howls, I wanted more.

I wanted *forever*.

He fucked me like it was the only thing that mattered, like the world was ending tomorrow, like we'd never have another chance.

He fucked me like he was saying goodbye.

Or maybe that was just in my imagination, knowing what I was about to do.

When he finally stilled on top of me, chest heaving, I felt the tears come again. I couldn't stop them.

Cole was catching his breath. "I'm sorry, Sunshine. I don't know what comes over me when I'm with you."

I was in love with Cole Jackman, and I always would be. But that didn't change anything.

I couldn't be my father's pawn anymore. I had to let Cole live his own life.

And there was only one way to be sure of that.

"Just one night?" The desk clerk looked up at me, snapping a wad of gum in the back of his jaw.

"Yes," I said, handing him my credit card. "Thank you."

I'd only been driving for a few hours, but exhaustion was starting to creep into my bones. This nameless motel on the outskirts of some farming town, just off the highway, was the best I could hope for tonight.

If I spent one more night in Alki, I might change my mind. But I couldn't drive any more tonight. I had to rest, clear my head, and start fresh in the morning.

The room smelled comfortingly musty. I collapsed on the bed and didn't move for several hours, until a loud pounding on my door roused me with a panicked jerk.

Heart pounding, I wished for a peephole in vain. It wasn't Cole - I would have known. And that only left one other option.

In spite of my better judgment, I opened the door.

My father looked up at me.

"How the hell did you find me?" I demanded, still blocking the door with my body.

"Lucky guess," he said, flatly. "Let me in, Heather."

There was no point in refusing. He could force his way in if he wanted.

"You followed me," I said, watching him flop down in the well-worn armchair by the TV.

My father sighed. "Princess, if I was following you, do you really think it would have taken me this long? One of my friends spotted you heading this direction. That's all I knew. I've been hitting up every motel along the way. Tedious as hell."

"Gosh, well, Dad - I'm sorry to have caused you so much trouble." I sat down on the edge of the bed, my arms folded tightly across my chest. "But I'm afraid this has all been a big waste of time. I'm not coming back."

"Cole must miss -"

"Don't you talk about him!" I shouted, my veneer of calm shattering. "Don't you dare say his name. You've done enough damage."

His face hardened, but he still wouldn't look at me. "Heather, you have to understand. These creatures are ruthless. When the bloodlust comes over him, you're just like prey. And the rest of the time, when he's wearing his human-suit and convincing you that he's in love - even if he means it, can you really trust someone like that?"

My jaw clenched. "He didn't ask to be what he is."

"And neither did I," said my father. "But we're both just trying to survive." His eyes moved in my direction, but his head didn't. "Whose side are you on, Heather?"

"There *are* no sides." I stood up, fuming. "Nobody except you and your stupid minions want there to be 'sides.'"

"There's so much more at stake here than you know." He reached into his pocket for something, but came up empty, frowning. "If you'd just trusted me from the beginning, and taken my word for it, this would be so much easier."

"*What* would be easier?" I demanded. "We're finished. This is over. I'm not helping you. I never was."

"Are you really telling me that you want to give up your sacred duty?" My father's voice grew even more bitter. "Your birthright?"

If I never hear the word birthright again, it'll be too soon.

"I can't listen to this," I said, turning away to pace the room. "If you don't leave, I'm calling the police."

"Don't you threaten me!" my father warned. "When all this goes down, you'll be sorry you turned your back on your old man."

"When all what goes down, Dad?" I demanded. "What exactly are you trying to do? I knew you weren't telling me the whole story before, but Christ. I don't know what you're talking about."

He was silent for a long while.

"Hello? Are you serious? Have I really got you at a loss for words, for once in your life?" I stalked over to him, stopping just a few feet away. "*What are you planning to do?*"

Finally, he lifted his face, meeting my eyes full-on. "Destroy them," he said. His voice was dead and hollow, filling me with a cold sense of dread. "Once and for all. Wipe them out. Leave one survivor to spread the news to the other clans, all over the world. We're sending a message. We're not gone, and we never will be. We're taking our world back."

The blood turned to ice in my veins.

"*What?*"

"You heard me," said my father, deadly calm. "If you'd cooperated with me, I would've let you pick the survivor. But honestly, I don't know if that's such a good idea anymore."

"You're joking." My lips felt numb. I wasn't sure how I was still talking. "This is - this is insane."

"Do I sound like I'm joking?" My father stood up, slowly, and headed for the door. "Don't worry. You're getting your wish now. I'm leaving. Now that you know what's at stake, you can make up your mind. Come fight with me, or run away."

He paused, with his hand on the knob.

"Or, of course, you can play the martyr and die beside your lover. But I've always thought you were smarter than that."

My father walked away, slamming the door behind him.

Chapter Nine

I sat there in silence for a long time, nothing but the ringing of my ears keeping me company. My father's words had left me gutted. I couldn't even begin to wrap my head around the depth of his treachery.

Using me was bad enough. Using me to fight a war, putting me in harm's way for the sake of his stupid vendetta…

I had to tell them. Even if Cole hated me for my betrayal, even if they didn't believe me, I had to try.

The drive back to Douglas Mountain felt endless. I sped the whole way, in silence, not even turning on the radio. My mind raced. I knew absolutely none of the details, but it didn't matter. I knew more than they did.

I didn't go to Steve and Andrea's. After the note I'd left, I didn't want to see them and have to explain why I was coming back, after all. Not yet, anyway.

There was someone I had to talk to first.

I pulled over and parked by the trailhead that was closest to the fountain. I knew instinctively that I'd find him there, sitting crosslegged on the ground, staring at the base of the fountain like it held all the answers to life itself.

He stood up as I approached, walking towards the woods on the other side of the clearing.

Whatever you're about to say, I don't want to hear it.

Now that I'd accepted the reality of hearing Cole's thoughts in my own head, I heard them loud and clear - almost more clearly that I heard my own.

"Please," I begged, taking another step towards him. "I need to talk to you."

"Heather, no." He turned away, keeping his eyes on the ground. "Please. For both of our sake's. Just stop this."

I let out a noise of frustration, running after him and cutting him off, but he just sidestepped me to keep walking. "Cole!" I shouted, inches from his face. He flinched, but didn't stop walking. "My father's trying to kill you!"

His feet froze. Slowly, he turned to look at me, his face haggard and haunted.

"*What* did you say?" His jaw twitched.

I stood tall, my fists clenched, forcing myself not to look away from his piercing eyes. "He wants to start a war," I said, surprising myself with the steadiness of my voice. "Like in the old days. He wants to wipe out the whole clan. He's found everyone who's left. All the warriors. He's one of them, Cole. And so am I."

His face was stony, but his chest rose and fell a little quicker, his nostrils flaring slightly with each breath.

"I wanted to tell you," I said, feeling a lump rise in my throat. "When I found out. But it sounded so ridiculous. And then I was afraid."

Cole's mouth twitched, but he didn't say anything. Didn't try to stop me, for which I was intensely grateful.

"At first, he said it was all about Foxwoods. Trying to get it back. He said they didn't have a right to the land, because of the treaty. I should have told him to go fuck himself. But I was in shock. I hadn't seen him in so long, and I…"

The lump took over momentarily, and I stopped, swallowing

hard.

"You realize," Cole said, finally, "that this all sounds completely crazy, right?"

I stared at him for a moment.

"You *turn into a wolf*," I said. "Can we set aside the judgments about what's crazy and what's not?"

He sighed. "Heather, I don't know what to think. You're talking about someone trying to start up a thousand-year-old war again. It's...it's beyond crazy, it just doesn't make any sense. I don't know what he said to you, but..."

"Listen," I cut in. "Remember all those things I told you, about the history of the war and the berserkers and everything? And you were so confused about why he knew all that? It makes sense. It's the only thing that makes sense. The way the animals follow me. The way you and I..."

His eyebrows lifted slightly, then furrowed. "Are you saying that us - that we -" He gestured vaguely. "Are you saying that's just because of your bloodline? The way I feel about you?"

It was the closest he was going to get, I thought - the closest thing to saying *I love you*. And there was no time for me to wrap my head around it.

"I don't know," I admitted. "I don't understand any of this, Cole, but I know that my father believes what he's saying. And I know that he meant it, when he said that he wanted to destroy all of you."

Cole raked his hands through his hair. "God damn it, Heather. I don't...I don't know what the fuck to think."

"Take me to Adanna," I said. "Let me explain it to her. I feel like...I think she'll understand."

He was watching me, carefully. Hesitating.

"I never wanted this," I insisted, taking a step towards him. "Please, Cole. Please. It's me. Every moment I spent with you, every time we..."

"Don't say 'made love,'" he warned, and any other time, he would have smiled. I felt a hysterical laugh bubbling up in my chest, but I held it back.

"Fine," I said. "It was all real. All of it."

Even though my father was trying to use me as a pawn.

Cole's face was beginning to soften. "And because you didn't trust me," he said.

"Yeah, all right, fine," I conceded. "Because you hurt me, and I was sure you were going to do it again. But mostly because I didn't want to hurt you. I didn't ever want you to be suspicious of me. I didn't want to see the look on your face right now, doubting everything we've had together."

Tears welled up in my eyes, and I couldn't swallow the lump in my throat anymore. Cole's face softened just a little bit more.

"Baby," he said, coming close and cupping my face in his hands. "I don't know what's going on, but I believe you. Okay? I know it was real. I can feel it."

He smiled a little.

"The rest of it, I don't understand. I won't pretend like it makes any sense. But we'll go talk to Adanna. We'll figure it out."

There was a sick guilt in my chest. Still, even with the clan at risk for their lives, I hadn't found a way to tell him. It didn't matter - except that it did.

He deserved to know.

And if I didn't tell him on my own terms, then my father would.

Adanna was sitting there in perfect silence, her face betraying nothing. I'd just finished telling her about my father's plans, and my throat felt like a desert.

"Why should I believe you?" she asked, softly. It wasn't a challenge, exactly, but she expected an answer. I swallowed with an effort.

116

"Because," I said. "If I was lying, I'd come up with something better than this."

She almost smiled.

"That's as good an answer as any," she said. "I thought this day would come, but I never thought I'd live to see it."

Cole leaned forward. "I thought this was over," he said, urgently, like he thought he could talk his way out of war.

"Things like this are never really over," said Adanna. "Sometimes they lie dormant. Sometimes for years. Decades. Centuries. But they're never over."

"So what do we do?" he wanted to know.

"First thing." Adanna sat up straighter. "We find the man responsible for this. We find Bill Alexander." She glanced at me. "Don't worry. We won't hurt him, unless he forces the issue."

"That's fair," I said.

"I already have Steve and Joe looking for him," she said. "They should be more than capable of bringing him to us. We'll find out as much as we can." She sighed. "And then, unless we can reason with him - we prepare for war."

I pinched the bridge of my nose, closing my eyes briefly, trying to wrap my head around everything. "Should you get - I don't know. Body armor? Something. What if they come at you with assault rifles?"

"They won't use assault rifles," said Adanna, calmly. "Weapons like that are…ineffective against us."

It took an actual effort for me not to ask about silver bullets.

"We have to be -" Cole made an unmistakable slicing gesture, his flattened hand sliding in front of his throat. "And we can only assume that they know that."

Oh.

"But *you* can use guns," I said, hardly believing what I was suggesting. "I mean - even if it's just for intimidation."

Adanna shook her head. "That's not how we fight," she said,

simply, in a tone that didn't allow for any discussion.

"Okay," I said, glancing from one to the other of them. "Well, in that case, uh…I'm all out of ideas."

"Don't worry, Heather," she said. "I know you want to help. And you have helped. But we can take this on. We've had to fight for our right to exist plenty of times, and we still have that blood running through our veins."

Adanna's office phone started ringing. She answered tersely, just nodding at first. "I understand," she said, at last. "Thank you."

Hanging up, she looked at me. "They've found your father," she said. "He's not hurt. They're bringing him here. If you want to leave, I'll understand."

"No," I said, quickly. "Please. I want to say something to him."

"Fair enough." Adanna gestured to both of us. "Come. We'll meet him outside."

My father looked like a sniveling, snarling animal, more so than any of the berserkers he was so desperate to eliminate.

Word had spread through Douglas mountain, either directly in directly, I wasn't sure - or maybe there were more mind-readers and empaths in this place than just me. Many of my neighbors had gathered around, staring at my father with accusing eyes, some yelling questions and invectives as Steve and Joe frog-marched him over.

"Just so you know, if you kill me now, my warriors are still coming," he shouted, as he approached. "The gears are moving. You can't stop this now."

Adanna stared at my father like he was a flea she wished to step on, but couldn't quite reach. "We have been at peace for centuries, Mr. Alexander. We have no desire to fight your people."

"I'll bring the war to your doorstep," my father snarled,

"whether you want it or not."

"Bill, you're being completely unreasonable." Joe's voice was strangely calm - almost *too* calm, I thought. A calmness that foretold much worse things ahead. "Sit back and think about what you're doing here. What you stand to lose. You're putting your daughter on the front lines of a conflict that you have no hope of winning. I don't know how many of you there are left in the world, but I know it can't be many. Not nearly as many as there are of us.

"You and I were friends, Bill. How many backyard barbecues did we have together? You can try to convince me it was all for show, but I know better."

"Friends!" my father scoffed. "Sure, you almost had me convinced that you liked me. Not that it matters. But I know what kind of person you really are. And all this time, you've been sniffing around my daughter like she's a dog in heat."

I'd never seen Joe so angry. His neck was taut, his head drawn back, both his hands clenched into fists. "I want you to think very carefully about what you're accusing me of, Bill. I've been like a father to Heather. Which is more than anybody can say for you."

My father twitched, like he was going to leap forward and attack. Both Joe and Cole stiffened in response, staring him down, waiting for a movement - and my father saw this, and stepped back.

He let out a harsh laugh. "You can sling arrows all you want," he said. "But it's not going to change my plans. Everything's already been set in motion."

"You're a fool, Mr. Alexander." Adanna's eyes flashed. "A dangerous fool. The blood of many people is going to be on your hands."

I couldn't stay silent anymore.

"Dad," I said, firmly, stepping forward. "Dad. This has to stop. You *have* to stop it."

He sneered at me. "Do yourself a favor, Heather, and stay out of things you don't understand."

I took one long, shaky breath.

"You're right, Dad," I said. "I don't understand a lot of things. I don't understand why you're doing this, and I don't understand why you can't just let go of this stupid vendetta. I wish I could stay out of it. But you've asked me to fight for you. You asked me to turn Cole against his own clan."

There was a quiet gasp, and murmurs from the crowd. My father's face blanched. I didn't dare look at Cole, but I could feel his gaze on me, dark and heavy.

"You believed Cole's loyalty to me could be more powerful," I went on. "And maybe it could. But I'll never find out."

I finally allowed myself a glance in Cole's direction. His face was in awe, his eyes burning with something that made my heart beat faster.

My father stared at me like I'd stabbed him in the chest.

"What are you saying, Heather?" he asked, hoarsely.

There was no turning back now.

"I'm saying that I won't fight for you," I said. "If you want a war, then bring it. But understand that you won't just be fighting the clan. You'll be fighting me."

Chapter Ten

As long as I lived, I'd never forget the look on my father's face.

He'd gone ashen, his mouth working open and shut a few times. But he had nothing to say. He's never thought, not for one moment, that I'd actually do it. That I'd fight on their side.

My father's hubris was always one of his worst qualities. And with him, that was saying something.

But the war was still coming. I hadn't expected anything different. Hell, I'd barely *hoped* for anything different. But he had to know. Even if it didn't make a difference, I had to say my piece.

We all made our way to the Foxwoods clubhouse for an emergency meeting, every single citizen of Douglas Mountain packing into the white-walled room with the fitfully rotating ceiling fan, and the purely decorative fireplace. It felt surreal, gathering to plan war strategies in a room with a built-in chess table and a kitchenette.

The energy in the room wasn't quite what I'd expected. Looking at the sea of faces, I thought I'd see confusion, hesitation, fear - basically everything I was feeling. But they were united in anger and determination. The young couple who'd spoken up during the first meeting were holding hands, tightly, their eyes hard and unyielding. Every face was the same.

Foxwoods, Alki Valley - for the first time in over a decade, it didn't matter.

Every single person in this room was ready to fight for their lives. For their land. I felt the thrill of it, thick in the air, and it made my heart beat faster.

The only one who seemed ambivalent was Arthur Craven. He lurked quietly in the corner, his eyes darting around the room, arms folded across his chest. He didn't seem like he was planning to speak.

I wondered about him.

No. He wouldn't. Not even Arthur would betray the clan.

I hoped my instincts were right.

"I need ten volunteers!" Adanna's voice echoed through the hall, and the quiet muttering died down. She was fierce, a fire burning in her eyes. "You'll run surveillance. Watch for the approaching army."

At least twenty arms shot up. Adanna assigned the posts, barking orders like she was born to be a general. Beside me, Cole's fingers twitched.

That should be me, he thought.

But instead of being laced with guilt, there was a hint of longing.

He *was* supposed to be the alpha. He just had to stop running from it.

"When they come, we'll be ready for them." Adanna was prowling the front of the room, hands behind her back. "Every one of us. To them, we're all the same. They don't care what neighborhood we live in. And now - neither do we."

The whole room broke out in a wordless cry that made my blood simmer in my veins.

I reached for Cole's hand, and he squeezed his acknowledgement, but he was a thousand miles away from me. He was seeing the battle, seeing himself leading the clan to victory.

As everyone began to disperse, I found myself gravitating towards Arthur. My empath qualities seemed to be the strongest around Cole, but I had a touch of it with all of them, I just couldn't ignore the anxiety radiating off of the neighborhood watch captain.

His eyes were hollow.

"I never thought I'd live to see war," he murmured. I wasn't sure if was talking to me. I wasn't even sure if he knew I was there.

"Neither did I," I said. "I mean - not this kind, anyway."

Arthur stared at the calendar on the wall, fluttering lightly in the breeze from the ceiling fan. "September twenty-third, two thousand and fourteen. War. Someday our children's children will remember this."

September?

Twenty-*third*?

SEPTEMBER TWENTY-THIRD?

Arthur shook himself off, and his prickly exterior quickly returned. But I hardly noticed. I was still staring at the calendar.

September twenty-third.

"Shit," I said.

"Well, that's the understatement of the century," Arthur said, turning on his heel and walking away.

He was right. But he had no idea *how* right he was.

I had to tell someone.

Not Cole. Absolutely not Cole. The last thing he needed to worry about, at a time like this, was whether or not I was...

I couldn't even *think* the word, let alone say it.

Ever since he came to town, ever since my father started this insane war, I'd more or less lost track of time. I hadn't even glanced at a calendar in so many weeks, as I drifted through this waking dream that was rapidly becoming a waking nightmare.

And now, I was *late*.

Not just fashionably late, either.

Adanna was the obvious choice. I knew that I could trust her, and she'd probably have some useful advice.

She'd already left the meeting, and I was able to slip away before Cole noticed me. I stole away to her office, and was relieved to see the desk lamp shining from the window.

When I knocked on the door, she answered quickly.

"I'm sorry," I said, immediately. "I'm sure you're busy."

"Not too busy." Her eyes were tired, but she smiled. "Never too busy for you. What's wrong, Heather?"

"I need to ask you something," I said, sitting down carefully. "It has nothing to do with the war. And I need you to promise you'll keep it secret."

"Of course," she said. "It would be a relief to talk about *anything* else."

Taking a deep breath, I bit my lips for a moment while I considered how to start. "I'm...I've been taking birth control pills for a long time. When Cole came back, I didn't think - well, I just figured everything would be okay. I didn't think I needed to be careful. I guess I should have."

Adanna's face grew serious. "Are you saying what I think you're saying, Heather?"

"I don't know," I admitted. "I haven't...I haven't taken a test yet. I guess I've been afraid to find out. With everything else that's going on, I couldn't even handle finding out something like that."

She nodded. "I understand," she said. "And I won't stop you from fighting, if that's what you want to do. But I want to be sure that you know I don't expect it. If there is a chance you're carrying a child, even a small chance, you have the right to protect yourself. And the baby."

Shaking my head, I tried to articulate my totally irrational feelings on the subject. "I have to fight," I said, finally. "Besides, it might be nothing."

"It might be," said Adanna. "It might be the stress, and the fear, playing tricks on your body. But I want you to understand what this means, if it *is* true."

My throat went dry. "And what is that?"

She was silent for a moment, playing with a beaded necklace between her fingers. "There's something peculiar about our people," she said. "And one of the reasons why there tend to be so few of us, compared to the commonfolk. For us, there is only one mate in the world with whom we can produce children."

It took a moment for this to sink in.

"It's always been like that," she went on. "In the olden days, they believed it was magic. They devised all kinds of rituals and spells to try and find true mates, but none of them were strictly successful. Some people still believe it's magic, but many think it must have something to do with undiscovered genetic markers. But no matter what you believe…it's not something to be taken lightly."

My head was buzzing. "I don't think I understand. So one of…one of your mates can be, uh, human? I mean, someone like me?"

She nodded. "From time to time," she said. "It's rare, but not vanishingly so. And I can't honestly say that I'm surprised. The connection between you and that boy - it's strong. I'm sure I don't have to tell you that."

"No," I said. "I guess you don't."

Smiling again, she reached over and patted my hand. "From the look on your face, I gather there's very little chance Cole is not the father."

"Very little," I agreed. "You might even say 'none.'"

"Your secret is safe with me," she said. Her whole bearing

seemed a bit lighter now, as if the thought of a new life starting had taken some of the edge off of the coming war. "But if you're afraid to tell him, you shouldn't be."

"What do you mean?" My breath caught in my throat. "I mean, I'm just - I know he cares about me. And I know I care about him. But honestly, I'm not sure anymore. I don't know what's happening between us. I'm not sure what his plans are. Unless you know something I don't." I looked at her, plaintively.

One corner of her mouth turned up. "You're not the only one I guard secrets for."

I had to respect that Adanna took people's confidence so seriously. But it was driving me crazy. Cole had obviously told her something about his feelings for me - something he certainly wasn't going to say to my face. Not the night before a war.

I went home alone after talking to Adanna. I kept checking my phone for a call from Cole, but it never came.

Then again, he had bigger things on his mind.

When someone knocked on the connecting door to Steve and Andrea's apartment, I nearly jumped out of my skin. They always gave me my privacy - I couldn't remember the last time one of them had actually knocked.

"Yeah?" I called out.

"Just me." It was Steve's voice filtering through the heavy wood. "I've got something for you."

I opened the door, welcoming him in. He was carrying something long and narrow, like a sword in its sheath. He sat down at the table, and I took a moment to be thankful that I'd covered Cole's gouges with some strategically placed junk mail.

"What's that?" I nodded at the object, which he was now holding in his lip.

"Here," he said, sliding it across the table. "We just use our teeth and claws, but you'll need something to fight with."

"Why do you have…" I looked down at the katana. "You know what, never mind."

His face broke into a tired grin. "At the time, it seemed like owning a sword would be very *metal*. I also had a pet scorpion."

"That's…that's amazing, Steve." I smiled, in spite of myself. "Never found much reason to use it, huh?"

"Nope," he admitted. "But you might."

Silence reigned for a few moments.

"Heather, I can't imagine what's going through your head right now," he said. "I'm not gonna pretend like I understand what it's like for you. But I do know everything's going to be okay. You're smart and you're strong, and so is Cole. You'll get through this."

I wasn't even allowing myself to think about the possibility that we wouldn't.

"Thanks," I said. "Can I ask you a question that's going to seem very strange, at a time like this?"

Steve chuckled. "Absolutely," he said. "No question is too strange on the night before a war."

"Adanna told me something earlier today. About the whole… thing." I made a series of vague hand gestures. "How there's, you know, 'one true mate' and they're the only person you can have kids with. I didn't really ask a lot of questions. But I guess she thinks me and Cole…" I drifted off. It felt too ridiculous, and too private, to put into words.

"Ah." Steve nodded, momentarily lost in thought. "Fated mates. They say everybody has one, but I don't know if I believe it. Most of us find a way to be perfectly happy with somebody we happen to meet. Just like everybody else in the world. But some people - yeah, some people spend a lot of time looking for their soulmate. They think it'll make them happy, if they find the perfect person. I don't know if we're any different from the commonfolk, in that regard."

I frowned. "So you don't really believe in it?"

"Oh, I believe it's real," he said. "For some people. For others, who knows? Me and Drea, we love each other. But we're not like you and Cole. That never bothered me. I knew I didn't want to spend the rest of my life searching for somebody I might never find. If my 'one true mate' showed up on my doorstep tomorrow, I'd send them packing."

He grinned.

"Love's not about some magical spark with the perfect person," he went on. "It's about what you decide to build together. Love's what you make of it. Nothing more, nothing less. You and Cole have something special. But you're going to have to work your ass off, if you want to be together - just like everybody else."

I stared down at the sword.

"That makes sense," I said. "Kind of."

Cole knocked on my door well past midnight.

"I'm sorry," he mumbled, not really looking at me. "Shit, Heather. I don't even know what to say."

I shook my head. "You don't have to say anything."

He took my face in his hands, staring at me like I was the best thing he'd ever seen - and like he was terrified he might never see it again.

"I wish I could talk you out of this," he said. "I wish you'd just stay the fuck away from the fight. If you get hurt, I won't be able to live with myself."

"I won't," I said. "But it wouldn't be your fault, anyway." A sick twist of guilt took over my chest. "He's *my* father."

Cole frowned. "Listen. Heather. Don't you *ever* feel responsible for him. None of this is your fault. He's delusional, and he saw his chance when the clan was too busy infighting to notice what was happening on the outside. None of that has anything to do with you. If you hadn't said something, he could have ambushed us in our sleep."

I knew everything he was saying was true, but I still felt like the worst person in the world.

"You were right," he said, after a long silence. "What you said, the other night, about how there's something else that scares me more than hurting you. But you were wrong, too. I'm not afraid of hurting you when I'm changed. I'm afraid of hurting you like *this*." He touched his chest. "*Here*."

"I know," I said. "And I can't tell you that's not going to happen. But I *can* tell you I'm willing to take that chance."

He sighed. "I've been an asshole, Sunshine. I thought I'd gotten better in the last ten years, but when I'm with you, I'm just a stupid teenager again."

In spite of everything, I was smiling. "I know what you mean."

"You deserve better," he rumbled, low in his chest. His eyes were starting to darken. Already, he was distracted by my proximity, by the feel of my skin under his hand. I knew, because I knew what he was feeling. And I felt it too.

I slid up close to him, winding my arm around his neck. "Maybe I don't want better," I murmured, against his mouth, before I kissed him breathless.

That night, we made love.

I'd never understood the difference before. He laid me down slow and gentle on the bed, feathering my body with kisses, every movement feeling like it took an eternity. When he finally slid inside, hard and unyielding, inch by inch, I made a long, low sound that I didn't even recognize.

Ever so slowly, he slid all the way out, and all the way back in. My body pulsed and quivered. When I looked in his eyes, like I had in the mirror, I didn't just see lust.

I saw love.

There was simply no mistaking it. Not anymore.

We stayed there for such a long time, locked in the dance, saying everything with our movements that we couldn't put into words. We kissed and kissed, endlessly, our bodies undulating. My pleasure came long and slow, shuddering, panting, my nails leaving long, deep scratches in his back.

We fell asleep together, the night before war, and I wouldn't have changed a thing about it.

Chapter Eleven

As I stood in the clearing surrounded by the clan, all wearing billowing cloaks - easier that way, Cole had explained, no clothes to get ripped or torn by the ones who shifted into something bigger - all I could hear was my heart beating in my own ears.

They were coming. They were coming any moment now, and they were ready for us.

Adanna's surveillance had paid off. We knew roughly where and roughly when, and we were ready. More or less.

As it turned out, it didn't matter. Miles before they arrived, we could all hear them. Marching, pushing through the underbrush, chanting something in an ancient language that I didn't understand.

That was supposed to be my destiny. But I'd chosen, instead, to stand with the people who'd been my true family.

And Cole, the only man I'd ever loved.

When the warriors came up over the hill, one single thought settled, heavy in the pit of my stomach.

There's so many more of them.

Their ranks went far back enough that I couldn't even guess at how many. Enough. Three or four of them for each one of us.

All armed, all trained, all angry.

I glanced at the others, at Cole, at Adanna, at Steve and Joe and everyone else I recognized from the corner store, from walks down the street, from the gas station and from the front counter at Joe's Automotive.

And they were afraid. Every single one of them felt the same sick terror as I did.

But they didn't move. Not once. They didn't so much as flinch.

I realized, as an afterthought, it was the first time I had actually seen their animal forms. Adanna transformed effortlessly into a huge, beautiful lioness. A few paces down the line, Steve shook his head a few times before he turned into a huge black bear, while Andrea became a sleek doe with smooth tawny fur. There were foxes, raccoons, even a mountain beaver. Joe became a badger, squat and angry. I struggled to take it all in, my eyes finally drifting back to the only one here that I'd seen transform before.

A massive shudder went through Cole's body as he began to change. I braced myself for the pain, but it felt so different than usual, a slow creeping ache, and my heart pounded, but there was no spiking agony. I stood still, watching him grow and change, while the enemy ranks shifted impatiently.

When it was done, Cole's black wolf eyes scanned the crowd. His nose twitched, his tail swished, and then, he threw back his head.

He howled. The sound made goosebumps rise all over, heating my blood. I wanted to snap my teeth and bite and scratch. I wanted to destroy them all, and mate with Cole on the freshly torn battlefield. I wanted to rip and tear and fight and fuck.

I just *wanted*.

Cole howled, and the warriors froze, fear in their eyes, no matter how hard they tried to hide it.

And chaos broke loose.

They advanced on us, swords and axes raised high, and the

clan charged forward. I tightened my grip around my katana, as ready for the fray as I would ever be.

The first warrior to take a swing at me was middle-aged and paunchy, not quite as intimidating as he'd seemed at a distance. I kept a wide stance for balance, parrying with my sword, pushing him back and off-balance. His arms windmilled comically as he fell over, his machete falling from his hand and skittering several feet away.

Well, how about that. Maybe that warrior's blood in my veins was actually good for something.

Pushing forward, I felt strong and fast and powerful in a way I never had before. Like I'd been waiting my whole life for a chance to do this.

How sick was that?

Everything seemed to be moving very slow, and very fast, at the same time. I'd lost all sense of how much time was passing, and at times I almost felt like I was floating above my body, watching everything from the sky above us.

It took a long time before there was enough of a lull for me to hesitate and look around me. As I did, my heart started to feel cold and heavy.

The clan was being beaten back. Slowly, but unmistakably.

Heather.

I looked around, as if I could hear the source of the voice. But I knew it was in my head.

And more than that, I knew exactly who it was.

Heather. Heather. Can you hear me?

I pushed one of the warriors off-balance with his own spear. Then, very deliberately, very carefully, I formed the word *YES* inside my head.

Good. Baby, listen. We need help. The animals are nearby. I can smell them. They're watching us. Tell them you need their help. They'll come for you.

I don't know how.

Yes you do. Just reach out to them. Same way you're reaching out to me now.

With as much energy as I could muster, while I continued to fight my way through the throngs, I brought up a picture of the cougar in my mind. The mother bear. Her baby. He must be fully grown by now. Every creature I'd seen during my solitary hikes.

Please come. Please help us.

Please help me.

If you want to keep the fountain -

A strange, unearthly roar came from behind me. I didn't dare turn to look, but I didn't need to. The ashen face of the man in front of me, suddenly dropping his axe and turning tail to run, told me everything. Moments later, a massive dark blur lumbered past me, shaking the ground. When it came to a stop, knocking over and trampling several of the warriors, it finally took definitive shape.

A grizzly bear.

He huffed and grunted, inches away from my face, and then lowered his head and shoulders in front of me. It only took me a moment to understand what he was offering me.

I climbed on his back, grabbing a handful of fur with my free hand. With a bellow, he charged forward, rearing up to swat the warriors aside like so many flies.

All around us, the animals were coming. Bears and bobcats, even the cougars - one of which had a scar across his face, and I had a halfway decent idea of who gave it to him.

But they were fighting for *me*.

They were fighting for the fountain.

I felt a rush of triumph as we charged across the battlefield. The animals leapt on the warriors, pushing them back, and the clan slowly started to regain their ground.

As my eyes scanned the crowd, I felt my chest constrict with sudden panic.

Cole. Where's Cole?

I reached out to him, silently, as the bear galloped across the field.

Sunshine…

In the back of my throat, I tasted fear.

My head jerked towards the further corner of the battlefield, and I saw him. Down on all fours, crouching, panting heavily with his ears flattened against his head.

And standing in front of him, with his battle-axe raised, was my father.

Why doesn't he attack? Why is he…

Then, I saw the glint of the silver chains that were holding Cole down.

No one had bothered to explain it to me, but I understood. The lore was true. It burned him, it robbed him of his strength. I could feel it.

I wanted to scream, but it died in my throat. The bear charged forward, but we were far, so far, and my father would hear the sound, and would he turn his axe on me? Would he ever hesitate?

Could I raise my sword to my own father?

He hauled his axe further back, and for a moment, the whole world froze.

And then I saw something I hadn't before.

Standing just a few feet away from them, sleeves of his pressed white shirt rolled up to his elbows, and his maroon tie wrapped around as a makeshift headband, was Arthur Craven.

I gripped the bear's fur, and he stopped, chest heaving. But we were close enough to hear my father's voice, now.

"I'm going to enjoy this," he intoned, his voice dripping with venom. "Did you ever stop think -"

"Excuse me," said Arthur. "But I'm afraid I can't let you do that."

One moment, he was standing there, fists clenched, grinning viciously - and in another, his clothes crumpled to the ground, and a massive crow flew out of his shirt collar.

With a screech, he flew talons-first into my father's face. The axe fell harmlessly to the ground, and my father flailed his arms helplessly while Arthur pecked and clawed.

I urged the bear forward again, hurrying towards Cole, jumping off and running towards him when I was close enough. The chains were heavy, and as I threw them aside, I saw the burning welts they'd raised on Cole's skin, even through his thick black fur.

Silence had fallen over the battlefield. As Cole straightened up, slowly, I surveyed what was left.

The few remaining warriors were on their knees, or barely standing, subdued by the clan and our animal allies. My father was groaning on the dirt, hands covering the scratches all over his face. Hovering over him, Arthur let out one single definitive *cawww*.

With a shake of his head, Cole shifted back to human form. Streaked with blood and sweat, eyes hard, he walked over to my father and loomed over him, fists clenched, chest heaving.

Slowly, my father opened his eyes.

The rest of the clan was slowly gathering around, some of them shifting back, slinging their cloaks back around themselves. Someone tossed Cole's to him, and he grabbed it out of the air, without looking.

My father was scrambling backwards on his elbows, his eyes filled with fear.

"This isn't over," he sputtered, his voice shaking. He managed to stand up, barely, his legs shaking.

"Look around you, Bill." Cole's eyes were like flint. "There's no one left."

My father's eyes skittered over the bodies of his fallen comrades, and he turned around, as if he expected to still see an army at his back. When he turned back, he saw nothing but us - the clan, slightly beaten and bloodied, but still upright. Still ready for more.

"Please, God," my father groaned, falling to his knees. "Jesus, no…"

"You can pray for His mercy," Adanna snarled, drawing herself high, seeming somehow to grow even taller. "But our gods are much older, and less forgiving."

For the first time in my life, I saw tears leak out of my father's eyes.

"So you find remorse on the brink of death," Adanna said. "Like all cowards." She turned to me, slowly. "Heather, if this man was anything but your flesh and blood, I would have already taken his head. Ask for mercy on his behalf, and there's not one of us who would go against your wishes." Her eyes narrowed as she turned to look at my father again. "No matter how much we might want to."

A fire burned in my chest, but no matter how much rage I felt when I looked at him, it was eclipsed by pity. Someone had twisted him, filled his mind with hate and fear, when he was too young to know any better. The same could have happened to me, if my mother hadn't stopped him.

"He should live," I said. "But far, far away from here."

Adanna nodded once. "So be it, Mr. Alexander - you've done one good thing in your life, at least. You raised a merciful daughter. More than you deserve. Now crawl back to whatever hole you came from, and if you lay one finger on another of my kind, I won't ask for her permission before I hunt you down."

Still weeping, my father tried to stumble to his feet. He stopped when I walked towards him, until I was close enough to bend down and whisper by his ear.

"You'll never know your grandchildren," I said. "Not that you'd want to, of course."

I stood up straight and tall, feeling as if a massive weight had been thrown off my shoulders. For the first time in my life, there was a lightness in my chest unburdened by memories.

There was just one burden left in the back of my mind, but it would be resolved soon enough.

I had to know the answer.

By some miracle, none of the clan had been seriously hurt. I never realized how resilient they were. In fact, in my ample view of Cole's naked back, I couldn't see the scratch marks I had left just hours before.

His kind healed fast. But some of the wounds were deeper, and needed attention. The clubhouse was our sanctuary. On the walk there, I deliberately fell back, staying out of Cole's eyesight, so I'd have a chance to answer a very important question.

Once we got there, before Cole could pick me out of the crowd, I disappeared into the bathroom with the pregnancy test that I'd been carrying around, unopened, in my purse.

I washed my hands carefully, just like the directions said - watching the blood and dirt swirl down the sink as my heart tried to escape from my ribcage.

Hands shaking, I tore open the wrapper, and prepared for the longest three minutes of my life.

Cole was standing in the middle of the room, looking lost. He'd pulled on his civilian clothes again, jeans and a faded logo tee, his muscles bulging under the sleeves. Any other time, my mouth would have been watering, and I'd forget what I was about to say.

But not now.

"There you are," he said, his face instantly breaking into a smile when he saw me. "Heather, I…" He stopped suddenly, seeing my face. "Heather, I'm sorry about…everything. Your dad, and…I don't even really know what to say."

I just shook my head, gesturing him over to a quiet corner where we could talk. "I need to tell you something," I said, my throat trying valiantly to close up. "Before you say anything else."

"What is it?" He leaned forward, worry etched across his face. "You're not hurt, are you?"

"No, no. Nothing like that." *Fuck.* My pulse pounded so loud I could hardly hear anything else in the room. Two simple words, that's all it was. But I couldn't find the breath to say them.

"Heather, please. Just tell me what's wrong." He was pleading, reaching out for my hands. I let him take them, rubbing them soothingly between his own, hearing the chatter of all the voices around me, the hum of activity, the sounds of bottles being uncapped and bandages being wrapped, in the makeshift infirmary on the opposite wall of the room.

Finally, the words forced their way out - almost of their own accord.

"Turns out, I'm pregnant."

I had to stifle a laugh at how stupid that sounded. Cole's face was frozen - white as a sheet, his mouth hanging open, his mind racing to process what he's just heard. But he didn't look upset. So that was a good sign.

"Heather," he said, finally, his voice barely above a whisper. "I…that's…that's…great, isn't it? Is it great? I mean, *I* think it's great. But you…" He swallowed hard. "You don't know what that means, do you? For people like us?"

"I talked to Adanna already," I told him. "Before I knew. I just suspected, but I had to talk to somebody. But she told me. She told me that it means we're…"

He was grinning.

"Cole," I said. "We're, I guess - soulmates, or whatever."

"I know," he said, simply. "At least, I've been pretty sure for a while now."

I frowned at him.

"I didn't know you'd get pregnant!" he said, quickly. "I mean, at least - I didn't even know it was *possible* until afterwards. By the time I realized what was going on, I'd already had ample opportunities to knock you up."

His grin was a little sheepish, now.

"You've got such a way with words," I said. "But how did you know? And why didn't you tell me?"

"How *could* I, Heather?" He took my face in his hands, his expression filled with so much tenderness and longing that it made my heart ache. "I wanted you to have a choice. Just because we're, you know, *connected* like this, it doesn't mean you have to be with me. It's your life."

"That's very noble," I said, "but you still haven't explained *how* you knew."

He cleared his throat. "There's all kinds of things," he said. "The way I feel about you, and the way it just overtakes everything else. I ignored it for a long time, until I couldn't anymore. The way you were able to keep me from changing all the way, when we fought. And even in the woods, when you needed - when you didn't want me to stop."

I blushed hotly. "I thought you were just feeling extra-passionate," I said.

"I was," he assured me. "But that's sort of a *thing*. The males of our kind, when their mate is in heat, there's basically no limit to what they can do. How long they can perform, and how many times, until their mate is satisfied."

Laughing, I bit my lower lip. "Interesting," I said. His eyes sparkled. "Good to know."

There was a moment of silence where all I heard was my heartbeat, and I tried to make sense of everything swirling inside my head and heart.

"Heather, I..." he paused, with eyes downcast, gathering his thoughts. When he looked back up at me, his expression was more guarded. "I know what you must be thinking. I know you've got no reason to trust me, still. But if you want me here, I'll be here. I'm never leaving this place again if I can help it. I can't stand the thought of it - of leaving you. But it's your choice.

"I want this. I want to be with you, I want to raise kids with you. I want to be able to reach out and touch you in the middle of the night, and hear you breathing, and know you're safe. But more than that, I want you to be happy. I want you to have what *you* want."

The answer was so simple. I felt light-headed and giddy.

"You," I said, watching his face slowly break into a smile again. "That's all."

He squeezed my hands tight, and I thought maybe it was the time to say *I love you*, but it seemed too trite and so shallow compared to how I felt. We'd said it a hundred thousand times to each other, as kids, when we hardly knew what the words meant.

"All this time, I kept having to remind myself that I wasn't your girlfriend," I said, shaking my head at my own stupidity. "I guess that should have been a sign that I was bullshitting myself."

"I don't want you to be my girlfriend, Sunshine," he said, softly, reaching up and brushing the side of my cheek with his thumb. "I want more than that."

My heart hammered in my chest. He licked his lips, nervously, I realized - he didn't want to put it into words. Because it was crazy.

But not doing it was even crazier.

"Say it," I whispered. "I need to hear you say it."

"I want you to be my wife."

We stared at each other, awed by what was passing between us. Even thought my heart leapt, what I felt most of all was peace. It was the feeling of walking into a warm house after a long walk in the snow, of seeing a light in a window from far away, and knowing that you'll be welcome there.

I wrapped my arms around his neck, and he pulled me close, smothering my laughter and my tears in the crook of his shoulder.

"Is that a yes?" he asked softly, teasingly.

"You didn't ask me a question," I pointed out, my voice muffled.

"True enough," he admitted. "Heather, baby, will you marry me?"

"*Yes*, Cole." I squeezed him tighter. "Yes."

Chapter Twelve

On the day I became Cole's wife, it was raining.

This shouldn't have been a surprise. Even with every forecast calling for one more unseasonably sunny day, fall had finally come in with a vengeance, and the skies had cracked open like an egg. "Torrential" barely began to cover it.

"Think we should build an ark?" Steve had his nose pressed up against the glass.

"Lived here his whole life, and still he can't stop bitching about the rain," said Andrea, affectionately. "Really, Heather - I'm sorry this happened."

I just shrugged, smiling. "I should've known better. An outdoor wedding in November? What was I thinking?"

We were all crammed inside Steve and Andrea's living room - everybody from Alki, and a few of the clan from Foxwoods. Arthur Craven, of course, had earned his invitation in battle. But even if he hadn't, having him there would have been less annoying than his complaining about *not* being invited.

Strictly speaking, it wasn't a wedding. The clan called it a "binding," but Adanna was qualified to sign the certificate for the state regardless, so the specifics didn't matter.

Cole had given me an idea of what to expect, but I was still terrified of doing something stupid. And I was more than a little disappointed about the rain.

I'd wanted to get married in front of the fountain, after all.

Even after everything I'd seen, I wasn't sure if I believed in magic. But if there was such a thing, the fountain was strong with it. I wanted its blessing.

Then again, I was pretty sure I had it either way.

Cole sidled up behind us. "Too bad about that weather."

"It's okay." I smiled up at him. "Sometime in the summer, we'll renew our vows at the fountain, and it'll be perfect."

He wrapped his arm around my shoulders. "By then, little Annabelle will be here to celebrate with us."

"Or Sebastian," I pointed out, with a grin.

"Yeah," he said, making a slight face. "We're gonna revisit that one."

Steve was frowning out the window. "Listen," he said. "That dripping sound. The rain's stopping."

"It'll be muddy," Andrea warned, following his train of thought perfectly. I had to smile. They might not be clan-sanctioned soulmates, but someday I hoped to be everything they were.

"So?" Steve shrugged. "Lived in the Pacific Northwest your whole life, are you afraid of a little mud?" He looked around the room. "How about the rest of you? Did you bring your rain boots? Or are you willing to sacrifice your fancy shoes to give Heather here the wedding of her dreams?"

They all broke out in cheers.

"I think you've been a little too loose with the mimosas, Steve," I said. "But, thank you."

"Come on!" Steve threw open the front door, gesturing to the guests. "Westward ho!"

We all tromped down in a procession, up to our ankles in mud, everyone laughing and chattering except us. Cole and I walked arm in arm, in a glowing silence. There was no "giving away the bride" tradition in binding ceremonies, which suited me just fine. I didn't belong to anybody except myself. But Joe and Steve had their place of honor, nonetheless.

"Thank you for not wearing a dress with a train," Andrea said, from behind me. "Seriously. I don't think I could handle keeping you out of the mud *and* not falling over myself."

"It's not *that* muddy," said Steve. "Might want to go easy on the champagne, darling."

As we got closer to the fountain, everyone fell silent.

The sense of peace and joy was spreading through the whole clearing. The fountain itself almost seemed to glow, I thought - a warm light bathing us in indescribable feelings.

Adanna wore a flowing dress of greens and browns, and a crown of daisies on her head. She smiled at us, the glow of the fountain surrounding and illuminating her.

"We're here today for the binding of Cole and Heather," she said, her voice even more musical than it usually was. "You will all bear witness to their promise to each other." She looked from one to the other of us. "Heather?"

I cleared my throat. "Many years ago, I stood in front of this very fountain and made a wish." I looked at Cole, his eyes shining, reflecting everything I felt but couldn't put into words. "Today, it's been granted. I suppose that was worth a penny."

The crowd broke out in soft laughter.

Cole's face was slightly awed as he looked at me. Like he'd wanted this to happen forever, but thought that it never would.

I knew the feeling.

Then, I said the words.

"I love you, I cherish you, I marry you."

Cole broke out into a grin.

"I made the same wish," he said, softly. "If you can believe that. It took the fountain a long time, but I think it finally managed to get our stubborn asses in line." He closed his eyes for

148

a moment, then opened them again, shining. "I love you, I cherish you, I marry you."

Adanna clapped her hands once. "So it is," she said. "For as long as you wish it."

We kissed in the light of the fountain, and everyone cheered.

And it was worth it.

Every little thing.

Every tear, every scar, every time our hearts broke for each other.

It was worth it.

"I have to say," said Commissioner Pollitt, smiling, with a trace amount of Steve's famous barbecue sauce smeared on her chin. "These are some of the finest ribs I've ever tasted."

"Plenty more where that came from!" Joe bellowed, from his post over by the grill. "Just say the words."

The commissioner shook her head, delicately dabbing at her face with a dollar store napkin. "I couldn't possibly. But thank you, all of you. Your hospitality means the world to me. Really."

"*De rien*, commissioner," said Cole, sliding into the seat next to her on the picnic bench.

"You speak French?" she asked, raising her eyebrows at him.

"*Un petit peu*. Not Quebecois, unfortunately, so there's probably a limit to how well we'd understand each other." Cole grinned. The charm was turned up to eleven, and Ms. Wanda Pollitt was certainly not immune. I noticed the blush traveling up her neck as she watched Cole finish off the bones on his plate.

"I figured it was only fair that you get a good look at the land, so you can make an informed decision," he said, when he'd finished sucking the lingering sauce off of his fingers. It had its desired effect on me, too; I sighed a little, remembering the last time I'd felt his tongue on my skin.

"I so rarely have the chance to visit out here," she confessed, looking around the table. "There just aren't enough hours in the day for me to do everything I'd like to. But when Cole stopped by my office with an invitation to a backyard barbecue, well…I couldn't resist." She smiled, her face turning pink. "Even though it took me a few months to get out here. I was determined to do it."

"Just in time for the first grill-up of the season," said Arthur, coming over with half of a hot dog doused in ketchup. "It's not technically a barbecue, you know."

"We all know, Arthur," said Cole, gesturing with a perfectly cleaned rib bone. "We just don't care."

"Well, whatever you call it, it's delicious," Arthur conceded, eating most of his hot dog in one bite. "I might have to re-think the Foxwoods policy on grills."

I couldn't help but laugh. "You really should, Arthur. Joe hardly *ever* burns his house down."

Hearing his name, Joe gave a jaunty wave with his spatula.

"Sure, sure." Arthur rolled his eyes. "You all laugh at me until something bad happens, and then who do you come running to? Good old Mr. Craven, who always keeps his head in a crisis."

"That's literally never happened." Cole grinned, flicking a piece of coleslaw in his direction. "I'd love to spend on a day on whatever delusional planet you live on."

"Fine," Arthur huffed, without any real malice. "But when your house actually *does* catch on fire, don't come running to me to re-write your community codes on the proximity of open flames."

"I'll be sure to keep that in mind," said Cole, raising his eyebrows at me. I giggled, sliding my feet further under the table to nudge against his.

"So," the commissioner said, "when can we see this impressive fountain?"

"Right now, if you're not feeling too stuffed." Cole stood up and came to my side of the table, offering me his hand.

"Are you sure you want to come along, Heather?" The commissioner eyed my stomach, which now stuck out far enough that it touched the edge of the table. "I'll understand if you'd rather not."

"Thanks, but I'm sure." I took Cole's hand and let him help me to my feet. "Got to keep active, while I still can."

And not leave you alone with my husband, I almost joked, but bit my tongue at the last second. It *was* just a joke.

Mostly.

As we hiked down the familiar path, I watched the commissioner's reactions. Her eyes grew wider as we walked, and she was amused and captivated by every passing bird and every squirrel that skittered across our paths.

She wasn't quite who I'd expected to meet, but then again, I'd been wrong before.

"I'm sure people will say I only came here for the photo op," she said. "But the truth is, all the objections I've been hearing about the land sale - well, they've made me wonder exactly what's so special about this place. The fountain, particularly. It's curious. I couldn't pass up the opportunity to see it with my own eyes."

Cole smiled, warm and mysterious. I wondered if he'd learned it from Adanna. "I promise, it'll be worth the trip."

The commissioner shook her head slightly, eyes on the ground as she walked. "If it was up to me, I'd keep every forest and every tree and every walking trail exactly as it is. But there's pressure. There's pressure on all sides, and trust me - it's not the kind that turns coal into diamonds." She smiled, wanly. "On paper, it's hard to defend keeping the land as state property. It's not generating any revenue, and it's not going to. Not everything is about money - except when it is, and every school system and library and the transportation department are all begging at your door. There just isn't enough to go around."

She slowed for a moment, taking in a deep breath of the pine-fresh air.

"Is it close?" she asked, her voice suddenly hushed. "Everything…sort of….feels different."

Cole nodded. "Just a little further."

The fountain was in full splendor today, almost as if *something* knew what was at stake. I was grateful for that. As much work as Cole had done, charming and coaxing her, and as euphoric as Steve's barbecue sauce and Joe's grilling was, ultimately, it was up to the fountain. We were counting on it advocating for itself.

I had a pretty good feeling about it, myself.

The commissioner was breathless.

Her eyes shining, she walked up towards the fountain, stopping a few paces away.

"Wow," she said, softly. "I mean…I've seen pictures, of course, but there's nothing quite like…"

"No," Cole agreed, winking at me. "There really isn't."

I went up to the fountain, resting one hand on my belly and the other on the white stone edge of the largest basin. The commissioner hovered nearby, just staring, a smile playing on her lips.

Cole appeared beside me, sliding his arm around my shoulders.

"Beautiful day for it," he said, softly. I smiled up at him. With the sunlight shining through his hair, casting little shadows across his face, he'd never looked more handsome.

The love of my life, my soulmate. The father of my little girl.

He rested his hand on my stomach, closing his eyes for a moment. I liked to pretend I could do what he did, but I couldn't. My gift didn't work with my own daughter, even as she grew inside me. But for some reason, even though Cole couldn't read my thoughts unless I projected them on purpose, he could read hers.

"She's so happy," he whispered. "Nothing but light and love."

"I wish things could stay that way," I murmured, looking down.

Cole rubbed his hand in little circles, and I felt Annabelle kick. Somewhere nearby, the commissioner was wandering across the pine needles, her eyes traveling up the massive tree trunks.

"We all used to be like this," he said, his voice filled with quiet awe.

Laughing softly, I stepped away from the fountain. "Maybe some of us," I said. "I find it hard to believe you weren't at least a *little* bit of an asshole in the womb."

He dropped a kiss on my forehead. "I think our brilliant plan is working."

"Hmm," I said. "Maybe we should take her out for ice cream to make sure."

Cole scoffed. "At this rate, Annabelle's gonna grow up with a vicious Ben and Jerry's addiction. You've got to control yourself, woman."

"You know what, when you're having the baby, you can decide exactly how much ice cream is appropriate," I said. "How's that sound?"

"Fair," he admitted, grinning.

I smiled and closed my eyes.

The sun shone down on us, bright and warm, as it had been shining down on the fountain since before any of us were born.

We did it, Sunshine.

We did it.

If you've enjoyed this story, please take a moment to leave a review. It lets me know what you'd like me to write more of!

Want to get exclusive content, freebies, special sales, and new release announcements? Join my newsletter: **eepurl.com/PaEAf**

You can also friend me as Melanie Marchande on Facebook: **facebook.com/melanie.marchande.3**, and Like my page as Lillian Danté: **facebook.com/lilliandanteauthor**. I love keeping in touch with my readers and hearing their thoughts. :)

If you love shifters and fated mates, check out this story from A.T. Mitchell:

Wish Upon a Tiger

NOTHING SEVERS FATED MATES. NOT

EVEN DESTINY ITSELF.

Jenna Argo never imagined she'd see Alaska for the first time as a prisoner. A ruthless treasure hunter's plot to use the curvy half-blood tigress as bait means a tragic first contact with her own kind.

Good thing Erik Nordclaw is smarter than human evil. Wild, strong, and deeply protective, this Alpha tiger shifter protects everything he claims. As soon as he lays eyes on the voluptuous angel, he knows saving Jenna won't be enough. Erik won't be satisfied until she's settled in his village and his bed.

Under her handsome savior's watch, everything makes sense for the first time in Jenna's life. A man to love and a place to call home are finally in claw's reach.

Then a devastating prophecy changes everything. Jenna's bloodline is cursed, and it's Erik's job to convince her otherwise, no matter how much a sinister scheme seems to confirm her dark fate.

Will determined Erik prove she's his fated mate, or will Jenna's prophecy doom him and all of Tiger Tree?

Note: This 38,000+ word BBW shifter romance contains love, war, and language that'll make a tiger growl. Dig your claws in. It's gonna be a wild ride!

❈ ❈ ❈

Available exclusively on Amazon Kindle:
smarturl.it/wishupontiger

10480221R00099

Printed in Great Britain
by Amazon